The Book of Changes

A Melanie Kroupa Book

The Book of Changes

Stories by

Tim Wynne-Jones

Orchard Books
New York

First United States Edition 1995 published by Orchard Books
First published in Canada by Douglas & McIntyre Ltd. in 1994

Orchard Books
95 Madison Avenue
New York, NY 10016

Manufactured in the United States of America
Book design by Chris Hammill Paul

10 9 8 7 6 5 4 3 2 1

The text of this book is set in 11½ pt. New Aster.

Library of Congress Cataloging-in-Publication Data

Wynne-Jones, Tim.
  The book of changes / stories by Tim Wynne-Jones.—
1st American ed.
     p. cm.
   "A Melanie Kroupa book"—Half t.p.
   Contents: The Clark Beans man—Madhouse—The
book of changes—Hard sell—The ghost of Eddy
Longo—Dawn—Gloria.
   ISBN 0-531-09489-8.—ISBN 0-531-08789-1 (lib. bdg.)
   1. Children's stories, Canadian. [1. Short stories.]
   I. Title.
PZ7.W993Bo   1995
[Fic]—dc20   95-6034

For my sibs,
Jen, Di, Wendy, Bry and G.P.

Acknowledgments

I like watching the credits at the end of a movie. Once they've thanked the dolly grip and the best boy, there are still lists of folks to acknowledge: rock sprayers and wig curlers and sandwich makers and the guy who helped Mr. Carpino get the keys out of his limo with a bent coat hanger. They try to thank *everybody*. I like that.

But it's so hard. I always forget someone. For instance, I forgot to thank Lissa Paul for her enthusiastic commentary on my last book before it was published. Thanks, Lissa.

I want to thank Brian Doyle for *Angel Square* and *Easy Avenue*. These are two books I put on like a pair of funny glasses to see my own past and the friends of my youth in a whole new way.

I want to thank Ian Tamblyn for the music "Kodiac Evening" on his record *Magnetic North*. It was a big piece of inspiration for the story "Dawn," as was my niece Emily Roach and her world travels. John and Heather Mallett were up for a long walk one day last spring, and "Gloria" grew out of that jaunt. And then there's Cam Grey, Franc Van Oort, Jim Deacove, Michael Nault and Bryce and Margo Bell. Thanks for being handy at the right moment.

Also, I owe a big hug to Magdalene Wynne-Jones, who was the first person to read these stories and whose opinion then and always means a lot. Thanks, Maddy.

No acknowledgment is complete without thanking Amanda, Xan and Lewis. But the fact is, no credit roll is ever truly complete. How do you thank a lifetime of friends, the things they do and the stories they tell you? And then there are those complete strangers who happen by with a coat hanger just when you've left the keys to your imagination locked in that stretchiest of all limos, your brain. Thanks! Thanks, everybody.

✑ Contents

The Clark Beans Man   1

Madhouse   24

The Book of Changes   47

Hard Sell   67

The Ghost of Eddy Longo   83

Dawn   109

Gloria   134

"Cohere," said a Stone in the church wall.

—From *The Once and Future King* by T. H. White

The Clark Beans Man

The night before Dwight started at a new school, his mother asked him to make a list of things he was proud of about himself. The list started off okay.

1. Can do excellent Donald Duck impression.
2. Memorized the names, positions and jersey numbers of every player on the Toronto Maple Leafs hockey team.
3. Draw monsters that make Vanessa cry.

That was as far as Dwight got.

"I'm sure you can name fifty other qualities about yourself," said his mother.

"Like what?" said Dwight. But she didn't have time to tell him right then, and besides, it was time for bed. He had a big day tomorrow.

So Dwight drew a monster to scare Vanessa with. It worked, but it wasn't very satisfying, since she cried all the time anyway. Dwight's mother reminded him that Vanessa was also starting at a new school the

next morning and that he might be a little more considerate.

Miss Milliken put Dwight in the second row from
the window near the back. She suggested that Nancy
could show him where they were in their math book.
Nancy didn't hear her. She seemed to be interested
in something going on outside the window, so Dwight
was forced to clear his throat and say excuse me a
couple of times.

"One hundred!" said Nancy.

"Thank you," said Dwight, turning to page 100.

"What?" said Nancy, turning to look at him. And
then before he could say anything, she gasped, turned
bright red and swore under her breath. One little
word. Four times.

Dwight touched his face, as if maybe it was covered
with marmalade or something.

Then the girl behind him leaned forward and told
him they were on page 230, not page 100. The girl
was giggling.

"What's going on?" said Dwight, looking over at
Nancy.

"She was counting convertibles," said the girl. "It's
a game we play. When you count to a hundred convertibles, the next boy you see is the one you're going
to marry."

Speechless, Dwight looked over at Nancy. Her face,
still crimson, was buried in her math.

"Is there any problem, Dwight?" asked Miss Milliken.

"No," he said. Except for the fact that he'd been in class fifteen minutes and he was already *engaged*.

In English later that morning, Nancy was asked to stand up and recite a poem the class was learning. It was written by William Wordsworth.

"I wandered lonely as a cloud," said Nancy, but as far as Dwight was concerned, she might have been wandering lonely as a bottle of cream soda. "I wandered lonely as a bottle of cream soda, that floats on high. . . ." To Dwight she didn't sound as if she was walking through a beautiful meadow filled with daffodils. She sounded as if she was sauntering through a mall.

"Good," said Miss Milliken enthusiastically when Nancy had finished. "You may add twenty-four lines to your bar graph, Nancy."

Nancy turned to the back of her English notebook and quickly topped up her bar graph. Dwight watched with some interest. Nancy had drawn a graph like a thermometer with a big star around 100. Apparently they had to memorize one hundred lines of poetry. Nancy was at forty-four.

Miss Milliken read another poem by William Wordsworth. It was called "The World Is Too Much with Us." It was a sonnet. Miss Milliken explained what a sonnet was, that there were fourteen lines in all and that in a sonnet like the one Wordsworth wrote there were eight lines in the first part and six lines in the second. She explained the rhyming scheme and that kind of thing. Dwight already knew about sonnets. It was good on your first day to find something you already knew.

Then Miss Milliken said everyone had to memorize "The World Is Too Much with Us" as part of their required memorization. Everyone groaned.

"You have a week," she said. The groans only grew louder. Undaunted, Miss Milliken continued, "I know the language is a bit strange to your ears, but it won't be once you've come to know it better."

The groans crescendoed and one big guy fell to the floor as if mortally wounded. Everyone laughed, including Miss Milliken. "Poetry never killed anyone," she said.

Dwight joined in the big groan session but just to be one of the class. Then a little guy near the front shot his hand up in the air.

"Yes, Kenny?" said Miss Milliken.

"I've been thinking," he said. "Can we learn more than a hundred lines of poetry? Can we learn as many as we want?"

"Oh, as many as you want. Yes," said Miss Milliken.

"Yes!" said Dwight under his breath. Nancy heard him and glared. She sure didn't want to marry someone who actually liked memorizing poetry.

"Because," said Kenny, leaning over his notepaper, scribbling away with a pencil, "if each blue line on the page represents two lines of poetry, you could get about sixty lines up the page, and if each bar was only about half an inch wide, you could get about ten bars across the page. You could graph about six hundred lines on just one page."

Everyone groaned again and said things like "Right,

Kenny," and "Here he goes again," and "Make it hard for us, Kenny," and things like that. But they seemed completely used to this kind of outburst from him.

Everyone but Dwight. He stared across the classroom at the guy making calculations in his notebook while everyone poked fun at him. A little tiny guy with the strangest croaky voice. The voice reminded Dwight of something Vanessa had made with a scrap piece of old lumber. She'd hammered a million nails into it and dolled it up with some aluminum foil and a rubber band and called it a boat. Kenny's voice was like that, a weird little boat. Full of purpose.

Then it was recess. Kenny came right up to Dwight in the school yard. (He came right up to about Dwight's shoulder.)

"We play two-handed touch football," he said. It was sort of like an order. "You can be on my team."

Dwight said yes, and the game started. They used a peewee-sized football, which seemed fitting because it was Kenny's ball. It was also Kenny's game, as far as Dwight could tell. Kenny's rules, too. Nobody seemed to mind except a big bear of a guy named Howie. The guy who had been mortally wounded by poetry.

"Get a life!" Howie would yell, just about every time Kenny made a pronouncement.

It was Howie who was guarding Dwight when Kenny unleashed a mighty throw down the sideline.

"I got it," yelled Howie, hurling himself at the ball. But the ball landed comfortably in Dwight's hands, and Howie landed not so comfortably on the chain-link fence.

"Run!" yelled Kenny in his rusty, rubbery voice. But Dwight wasn't sure if he should.

Howie groaned as if in pain.

"Are you hurt?"

"Forget about him!" screamed Kenny. "What are you doing? Run! Are you crazy?"

Suddenly Howie, still on the ground, kicked out savagely and smashed Dwight square in the knee. "Gotcha," he said, grinning ferociously. Dwight buckled from the kick.

Kenny arrived on the scene, breathless. "Give me the ball," he demanded. Dwight tossed him the ball, glad to be rid of it.

"It's dead," said Howie.

"Touchdown," yelled Kenny as he crossed the line.

"The ball's dead!" yelled Howie. "I touched him, you freak."

Kenny ran back. "It's two-*hand*ed touch," he said. "Not one-*foot*ed touch."

"Get a life, moron!" yelled Howie.

Then Howie and Kenny yelled at each other and pushed each other until the bell. The rest of the teams wandered off, but Dwight watched with interest. Kenny came up to about Howie's chest, but he didn't seem bothered by the big guy.

The game resumed at lunch and in the afternoon recess. So did the argument. Howie was huge and dangerous-looking. It amazed Dwight to watch Kenny take him on. Like a little Jack Russell terrier, yipping and nipping at a bear.

Dwight walked home through the park, reading Wordsworth's sonnet—he already had the first eight lines pretty well down pat. With his head in the book, he didn't see the bear until he walked right into him.

"Whatcha doing in my park?" said Howie.

Dwight was so surprised, he actually believed for a second that he had somehow wandered lonely as a cloud into someone's backyard. Howie made a grab for him, and Dwight danced out of his way, losing his English book as he did. It fluttered to the ground. Howie slid into the book as if it was second base, just as Dwight picked it up again. He got a scrape on the hand from Howie's foot and got away with another kick on the leg.

Lying on the ground, Howie laughed, as if he had won some kind of contest. This was his game and his rules. Dwight ran the rest of the way home. The first eight lines of the poem got all jiggled up in his brain, and it took quite a while to sort them out again.

He didn't tell anyone about the attack, but he drew a great monster with fat lips and too many arms and jackhammer legs. Vanessa hated it so much that she tore it up in little pieces. Which was fine with Dwight.

The next day, Dwight approached Miss Milliken when the class was dismissed for lunch.

"When can we recite 'The World Is Too Much with Us?'" he asked, quietly so no one passing by would hear.

Miss Milliken smiled delightedly. "It's not due until next week."

"How about right now?" said Dwight. It wasn't a poem he planned on holding on to, if he could help it. And he wasn't going to recite in class any poem that had the line: "This sea that bares her bosom to the moon."

Miss Milliken sat down and crossed her hands. "Shoot," she said.

Dwight recited the poem.

"Word perfect," said Miss Milliken. From the satisfied little look on her face, Dwight gathered that she liked Wordsworth more than he did.

"So I can start my bar graph?" he asked.

"You certainly may."

"Do I have to learn the cloud poem the class already did?"

"Not really," said Miss Milliken. "But I doubt it would present you with much trouble."

"No," said Dwight. "No trouble. But if we can learn anything we like, it seems pretty short to me."

Miss Milliken chuckled. "Well, at last Kenny Finnigan is going to have some serious competition."

"I've got some catch-up to do."

"True," said Miss Milliken.

"But at least I beat him with this one," said Dwight proudly.

"Almost," said Miss Milliken. "Kenny was in first thing this morning."

They played touch football at lunch and then at recess. It was Kenny's ball and Kenny was always captain and he always chose Dwight. He chose him first, though there were much better players. He never chose Howie. He liked to yell at Howie. He liked to yell at everyone, but it was more fun yelling at someone when they were on the other team.

Kenny could pass the ball a long way, considering his size. He would kind of coil himself up like a spring and launch the thing with his whole body.

"Go long!" he'd yell at his teammates in his croaky voice. "Go long!" To Kenny, every play was a must play—the last chance to score. Every play was in danger of being interrupted by the bell.

Dwight was so busy staying out of Howie's way that he flubbed a lot of catches that day. He didn't say anything about what had happened in the park, but it was on his mind. He couldn't tell if it was on Howie's mind. It was hard to tell if anything was on Howie's mind.

That afternoon, Miss Milliken announced to the class that although they still had most of a week to get their poem memorized, two students had learned it overnight. She didn't say who. Everybody assumed Kenny, and, by a process of elimination, the rumor mills soon pegged "the new kid" as the other likely suspect. Nancy, at least, was convinced it was him. So was Howie, who shoved his finger down his throat a few times to show Dwight what he thought of kids who learned poems overnight.

And Kenny was convinced. He stared across the classroom with new interest in Dwight.

When the class had a free period that afternoon, Kenny wandered back to Dwight's desk. When Nancy saw him coming, she turned away in disgust. "Oh, my *gawd*," she murmured.

"What's wrong with her?" Kenny asked, leaning on Dwight's desk.

Dwight shrugged.

"Oh, my *gawd*," said Nancy.

But Kenny wasn't really interested in Nancy. He hunched forward and lowered his voice. "What are you doing next?" he asked.

"What do you mean?"

"Get off the pot!" said Kenny. He had such a gleam in his eye, Dwight gave up trying to pretend he wasn't the phantom memorizer.

"I dunno," he said.

"Come on," said Kenny, smiling a crooked smile. "You tell me and I'll tell you."

But Dwight didn't know yet and he said so.

Kenny looked hard at him. Dwight didn't blink. Kenny sighed. "If that's the way you want it," he said. "But this means war."

After school Kenny caught up to Dwight walking east along Gladstone. He tapped him on the shoulder, and Dwight jumped out of his skin.

"Nervous, eh?" said Kenny.

"You just surprised me."

"Huh!" said Kenny. "You're scared. Admit it."

Dwight was. And he was just about to tell Kenny about Howie's attack in the park when Kenny suddenly burst out, "Okay, okay. I'll tell you what I'm learning: 'The Charge of the Light Brigade.' Ever heard of it?"

Dwight shook his head, momentarily confused.

Kenny smiled wickedly.

> *"Theirs not to make reply,*
> *Theirs not to reason why,*
> *Theirs but to do and die.*
> *Into the valley of Death*
> *Rode the six hundred.*

"Fifty-five lines in all," he said. "Beat that!"

Dwight lost his nerve. How could he explain to someone like Kenny that he was afraid of Howie? Kenny—all two foot nothing of him—was fearless. At football. At memorization. At everything.

They parted at Fairmont, and Dwight headed south, but he didn't take the opportunity to peruse his English textbook for large poems. He kept his eyes peeled for large bearlike boys with large bearlike tempers and small wormlike brains.

He got almost all the way across the park before Howie got him—got him from behind. He'd been lying in wait. He jumped out of the bushes and tackled Dwight with a shout of glee.

"Leave me alone," said Dwight, writhing on the ground, trying to get himself free.

"Leave me alone," aped Howie, sitting on Dwight's chest, pinning his arms down with his knees. Dwight gave up and lay on the hard ground, waiting for whatever was going to happen next.

"This is for pushing me in the fence," he said. He made a big horking noise.

"I didn't push you in the fence," said Dwight. He turned his face away just as a huge gob of spit landed on his cheek.

Howie's laughter was cut short, however, because suddenly there was a kamikaze scream from behind them and a peewee football came hurtling though the air and hit Howie square on the back of the head.

"Hey!" said Howie, losing his grip on Dwight, who immediately started to struggle free.

Kenny came running toward them and scooped up the ball where it was bouncing around on the ground.

"Get off him, you big fat lummox," he yelled, and beaned Howie with the football again.

"Cut it out," yelled Howie, covering his head with his hands. Dwight dragged himself out from under Howie, who was clambering to his feet.

Meanwhile, Kenny had retrieved the ball again. "Catch," he said, and he threw it at Howie, who caught it.

"Throw it back," said Kenny, jumping about like a crazy target.

"You stupid nerd-for-brains," yelled Howie. But— and Dwight couldn't exactly understand this—he threw the ball back to Kenny.

Kenny immediately took his quarterback stance.

"Go long!" he yelled. "Go long!"

"Forget it," said Howie.

"Go long!" shouted Kenny, and there was an urgency in his voice, as if it was the last chance in the game and they were one touchdown behind and it was all up to Howie to save the day. Dwight turned in amazement to watch Howie suddenly take off, fading

long down the field: twenty, thirty, forty yards, waiting for the big bomb that would win the day.

"Are you okay?" muttered Kenny under his breath.

"Yes," said Dwight, wiping the spit off his face.

"Get ready to run," he said. For Howie had stopped, realizing, too late, that he'd been had.

"Now!" said Kenny. And, tucking the ball into his pocket, he started running, with Dwight beside him, leaving Howie ranting with rage like some gullible giant in a fairy tale.

They tore down a path that skirted the playing field until they came to a concrete tunnel through the hillside. It was dark and the ground was muddy. They splashed on through. On the other side, Kenny veered suddenly off the track and up the steep slope into the trees, with Dwight right behind him. He was pretty sure Howie hadn't followed, but he was running now for the sheer exhilaration of escape.

They came out of the wooded hillside at a narrow street of little houses, out of breath from the climb, but still not ready to quit the adventure. Halfway down the block, Kenny once more veered down an alley. He was five strides ahead of Dwight when he cut behind a Dumpster that sat out back of a long, low office building. Out of view, they stopped at last, panting heavily, and leaned against the yellow brick wall of the building.

"Thanks," said Dwight, when he could speak again.

Kenny smiled triumphantly. "I started thinking about how jumpy you were," he said between big breaths. "Then I figured out which way you went home and I thought, ah-ha!—Howie!"

"Amazing," said Dwight.

"No," said Kenny. "Experience. He used to get me in that park, too."

For some reason, Dwight was surprised to hear of Howie intimidating Kenny, let alone beating him up.

Kenny pulled a stick of Juicy Fruit from his jacket pocket. He fished around for another one.

"Where do you live?" he asked. Dwight told him. They were almost neighbors. Then Kenny told him how to get home without going through the park. He used the stick of Juicy Fruit like a conductor's baton, as if he was drawing the way home in the air. Dwight watched the little yellow baton and listened carefully.

There was no more gum in Kenny's pocket, so he tore the one stick in half.

"There are two kinds of bullies," he said, handing one half stick of gum to Dwight. "The kind who beat you up in the school yard for attention, and the kind who beat you up in secret."

Dwight unwrapped his half piece of gum thoughtfully. "Howie's the second kind," he said. "He only shoves a bit at school and acts tough."

"Right," said Kenny. "The secret ones are dangerous."

They chewed in silence for a minute.

"He doesn't bug you now," said Dwight.

Kenny nodded.

"You've got to think of something—some kind of diversion—with a guy like Howie," he said. "I read somewhere that the movie director Steven Spielberg kept getting beat up by this bully at his school. Spielberg made movies even when he was a kid. So he went up to this bully one day and asked him if he'd star in his next flick. The bully said yes, and became the hero of the movie. And that was that. They became friends."

"Cool," said Dwight.

"I tried it with Howie."

"You did?"

Kenny nodded. "Yup. He liked the idea of being a movie star. There was only one problem."

"What?"

"I didn't know how to make a movie."

"Oh," said Dwight.

"I didn't have a camera. No story, not even an idea—nothing."

"So what did you do?"

"I started taking the other way home."

The sweet taste of the gum that had filled Dwight's mouth seemed to wear off pretty quickly. Only half a stick. What could you expect?

"It worked anyway," said Kenny. "Well, kind of. While he thought he was going to be a movie star, he didn't beat me up anymore. It kind of broke the pattern."

"But when he found out—?"

"He never really found out. I mean, I never actually told him I *wasn't* going to make a movie. I just started taking the other way home."

Dwight thought of Howie in the park waiting day after day for Kenny to come. He tried hard to imagine a kid as stupid as Howie.

"The thing is," said Kenny, "he's going to get you every day in the park until you're not there to get. But once he doesn't get you for a few days, he'll probably forget about it. Or find somebody else."

Dwight nodded. Then he sighed. He had dared to hope that cocky little Kenny could teach him how to stop Howie from bugging him. Not just how to avoid him.

Kenny clapped Dwight on the arm. He had a cracked kind of smile on his face. "Good things happen when you take a different way home," he said. "I'd never have found this place if I hadn't been trying to get away from Howie."

"This place?" Dwight looked up at the wall he was leaning against. It had just been a good wall to lean on until then.

"Come here," said Kenny.

He dragged Dwight along a bit until they came to a large window. The lights were on inside. They looked down into a basement room with a tiled floor and brightly painted walls. An art room. They leaned against the glass. A man inside was drawing at a big drawing table. Behind him there was a door with a red light over it. On the light were the words ON AIR. The light was on. It was a studio of some kind.

"Threshold Studios," said Kenny. "They make cartoons."

The artist was painting a little man in a sailor suit. Dwight had seen the cartoon man before. It was the Clark Beans man from the commercials on TV. Beside the artist was a thick wad of pencil drawings of the Clark Beans man.

When the artist paused in his painting, Kenny tapped on the glass.

The man looked up. He smiled and waved at Kenny.

He got up from the table and stretched. He placed his paintbrush carefully in a water glass. He came over to the window, waved at Dwight. Dwight waved back.

Then the artist took a thick marker from his pocket and wrote on the glass in big comic-book-style letters, "Hi ya, guys. How yez doin'?" He turned the question mark into a worm with his head pointing down, recoiling in horror at the period underneath him, which was a hungry-looking face with big teeth. That period was going to eat the wiggly part of the question mark right up. The boys laughed.

To Dwight, the most remarkable thing was that in order for them to read the words, the artist had to write backward, and yet it didn't seem to slow him down at all. Dwight was convinced that he was in the presence of a genius.

And the show wasn't over yet. The artist went over to his desk and grabbed the thick wad of pencil drawings. He held them up to the window and flicked them so that the little Clark Beans man seemed to pick up a spoon as big as himself and dig into a bowl of beans. The artist did the flip book a couple of times. Then he got a second one from beside his desk and flipped the pages in it. Now the Clark Beans man was pole-vaulting right over the bowl. Well, almost. He didn't make it and landed *KERSPLASH*! in the middle of the beans. It was brilliant.

The boys clapped. The artist bowed and waved good-bye, pointing at his watch and making chopping gestures at his neck. He was going to get it bad if he didn't get the Clark Beans job finished soon. He went back to work.

The boys leaned against the glass and watched him for about a year. Luckily, time stood still, so their parents didn't report them missing, and they didn't get hungry or anything. Not much happened, really. The Clark Beans man gained a blue shirt and a painted-on smile. Then another artist came in to discuss something, and that broke the spell. They could leave.

When Kenny and Dwight went their separate ways at the end of the block, Dwight made his way home thinking that getting beat up had almost been worth it.

Almost.

He took Kenny's advice for the rest of the week and walked home the long way around the park. Howie never said anything about it at school. It was just as Kenny had predicted. It was as if Howie didn't even think about beating you up if you weren't there. Or maybe it was only when he was in the park that something came over him.

One day after school, Dwight went to the public library and asked the librarian for a book with some good poems in it—adventures, if there were any. They found a book of narrative poems that had "The Charge of the Light Brigade" in it, so Dwight settled down with that.

He liked "The Charge of the Light Brigade." It was exciting. But then he found "The Shooting of Dan McGrew" by Robert Service and, as far as he was concerned, it was better. For one thing it took place

opped, but not because he cared about
ines there were in a sonnet. Dwight had
take, a whole bunch of mistakes. Daring
park had been his first mistake. Thinking
Howie and he could be friends had been
mistake. And calling Howie an idiot had
mistake. Without Howie saying a single
t could see in his eyes that he'd gone too
l feel Howie's anger turning to stone on
ere wasn't anything he could do.

ere?

ne too far? Or had he just not gone far

teen, you idiot!" he shouted again. But
shouted it in the voice of Donald Duck.
ked at him in amazement.

't you know nothin' about poetry, you
or-nothin' excuse for a stump!"

s looking at him strangely. Strangely
me as nastily. And so with great force
only muscle not pinned down by the
of Howie the bear, Dwight began to
worth's "The World Is Too Much with
ice of Donald Duck.

transfixed. Transfixiated. Rendered mo-
his years of beating up nerds, no one had
petry to him in the voice of Donald Duck.
ld feel the body over him relax. But it
e started "The Shooting of Dan McGrew"
ctually laughed, and he was halfway
fore Howie actually leaned back on his
eing Dwight's arms. Dwight could have

in the Yukon. But, most important, it was fifty-eight
lines long—three lines longer than Kenny's poem. He
started learning it right away.

Kenny was already at 80 lines on his bar graph, and
"The Charge" would take him up to 135. So Dwight
decided to learn "The Cremation of Sam McGee" as
well. It was also by Robert Service. It was 68 lines
long, with eight lines thrown in for free because the
first bit got repeated at the end. Along with the Wordsworth sonnet, he'd be up to 140. Kenny might have
had a head start, but that only made Dwight work
harder.

When he recited "The Shooting" one morning before class, he asked Miss Milliken not to tell Kenny;
he wanted it to be a surprise.

Very carefully he colored in the rising mercury on
the poetry thermometer at the back of his notebook.
He'd done the Wordsworth in red because he was
thinking of the bar graph as a thermometer. But he
decided now to do each poem in a different color. He
did "The Shooting" in black. And he was going to do
"The Cremation" in fire-bright orange!

He recited "The Shooting" on the Monday of his
second week at school. He spent the long way home
working on "The Cremation." By the end of the week
he wanted to be neck and neck with Kenny.

When Dwight stopped to think about it later, he
wasn't really sure why he walked through the park
Tuesday after school. He hadn't forgotten about Howie. But Howie, apart from yelling a lot when they

were playing ball at recess, didn't seem so dangerous anymore. Partly it was that. But partly it was also that Dwight was angry at having to go the long way home. He had dropped by Threshold Studios a couple of times, and the artist always said hi and drew little cartoons on the window, if he had the time. It was great. But Dwight wanted to *choose* how he got home. So on Tuesday, he chose to go home by the park. He was faster than Howie. It would all be fine as long as he was prepared.

It was a sunny day. The park looked empty. Dwight walked quickly, keeping his eyes on the bushes where Howie had surprised him before. He glanced around a few times to make sure Howie wasn't sneaking up on him.

He was most of the way across the playground when he heard a car door slam. He looked over. Somebody had stopped to let off a passenger. The passenger was Howie. He waved at Dwight, as if they were friends. Were they? Or was it just a show for the driver of the car? His mother, perhaps.

"Oh, Mom, there's my new pal Dwight. Mind if I walk the rest of the way home?"

Dwight waved back, but he didn't stop. Just a little wave. It was possible. He wanted to believe it was possible. They only lived a block apart. They played football together every recess. What's more, Kenny had said all you had to do with someone like Howie was break the pattern.

"Hey, wait up," called Howie.

Dwight slowed down a little. Friends? It made sense

to have someone
as an enemy.

Howie was get
of friendly way, n
Was it possible?

"Hi, Howie," h
look back toward
And when Howie
was nothing like

It was too late
but again Howie
his books a coup
bear growl. How
them away. Then
pinned his arms t

He laughed. "T
nerd-for-brains tr

Flicking his in
pinged Dwight in
"Ow!"

"That's for trick

"I didn't trick y

"And here's sixte
stupid poem."

"Ow! Ow!"

Howie laughed

Dwight was fur
going too far!"

"Why should I?"

"Because there a
you idiot!"

Howie s
how many
made a mi
to cross th
that maybe
his second
been his la
word, Dwi
far. He co
his chest.

Or was

Had he
enough?

"Only f
this time

Howie

"Jeez! I
crazy, go

Howie
wasn't th
and with
hulking
recite We
Us" in th

Howie
tionless. I
ever recit

Dwigh
wasn't u
that Ho
through
haunche

socked him in the face—he was mad enough to. But he was scared enough not to. The poetry didn't work as fast as a punch, but the consequences looked more hopeful.

He was exhausted when he finished "The Shooting."

"Can I get up now?" he asked.

"Say it in the duck voice," said Howie cheerfully.

"Can I get up now?" said Dwight in the duck voice.

Howie suddenly leapt up and held out his hand to drag his limp victim to his feet. He even chuckled as he dusted the grass and leaves off him. He quacked himself a few times. "How do you make it come out in words?" he asked.

"It's an old family secret," said Dwight.

"Cool."

Dwight wanted to run now that he was up, but his limbs all felt like jelly. "Walk me home, you stump-for-brains!" he shouted at Howie in the duck voice. Howie laughed and punched him in the shoulder. Affectionately.

They walked in silence for a few minutes. Gingerly. Dwight was afraid that at any minute, Howie was going to come to his senses. But as they walked along and home got closer and closer, he realized that Howie really didn't have any senses to come to. Dwight had won. Round one, at least.

He waved good-bye to Howie at Howie's place and was moving on up the hill to his own house when Howie called to him. Dwight turned with some trepidation.

"Hey," said Howie. "You should be in Kenny's movie."

☙ Madhouse

Solly came down the stairs with his laundry hamper. He was supposed to have done his laundry the night before, but there had been a band practice. He was hoping to get something washed and dried in time for school; otherwise he'd be going in his pajamas.

He stopped on the stairs a minute and tried to imagine everyone at school in pajamas: the principal, Mr. Dent, in a threadbare old dressing gown; Mr. Schmeitzer, the gym instructor, in a flannel sleeper with little football players all over it and a trap door in the rear; Ms. Beattie in something filmy and flimsy like a movie star. They'd all forgotten to do their laundry. It was declared pajama day.

"Why are you standing on the stairs?"

It was D'Arcy. She was at the table fiddling with an egg.

"What are you doing with that egg?" asked Solly.

"It's the autumnal equinox today," she said. "If the heavens are aligned, an egg will stand on its end."

"Not in this house," grumbled Solly.

He thumped his laundry hamper down the stairs, losing socks the whole way. All he knew about the equinox was that the day was as long as the night. And from now on the days would grow shorter. But it would be great if the egg would stand on its end. Could such a thing really happen?

He stopped at the table and watched for a minute. Nothing.

Solly dragged his hamper through the kitchen toward the laundry room. There was no wall between the kitchen and dining room, just an island littered with phone messages, drawings, magic markers, and orphaned dishes. Solly's seven-year-old brother was sitting on a stool at the island eating frozen peas.

"Hi, Solly," he said. Peas fell out of his mouth and rattled on the floor.

On the stove the kettle was boiling. The top started whistling.

"I'll get it," said Solly's mother, as if it were a phone call. But she was in the living room playing the guitar, so Solly stopped and made the tea. Solly was the only kid he knew whose mother took electric guitar classes. Her class was right after his. He had tried to stop her. "It's an invasion of privacy," he had said.

"Ah-ha!" his mother had answered. "Why don't you name your group *Invasion of Privacy?*" Solly's rock band had been looking for a name for months. His family was always giving him ideas. At the fall fair they had been watching a livestock competition because D'Arcy's jumping event was next. The livestock competition was called *Mares with Visibly Nursing Foals*.

"That's it!" Solly's father had said. "Can't you just see it on 'MTV'? *Solly Henson and the Visibly Nursing Foals."*

Boz had been with them at the time. He was Solly's best friend and the lead guitarist in the band. "It isn't *my* band," Solly had said. His parents could be so embarrassing.

Solly poured the water into the teapot, splashing his naked foot.

"Ow!" He danced around the kitchen.

"Why don't you name your band *Autumnal Equinox?*" said D'Arcy.

"Never mind," said Solly, dragging his hamper into the laundry room.

"Why don't you call the band *Never Mind?*" said the seven-year-old, his mouth full of peas.

Solly shut the laundry-room door behind him. The band already had a name, as of last night. He turned on the washing machine and let the noise of the water filling the tub block out all the good ideas coming from his ever helpful family. He scooped up a cup of detergent and began pouring it into the machine. He had emptied half the cup before he realized there was a wash still in the tub. A finished wash. Earl's wash. Earl never remembered to put his washing in the dryer.

Solly punched the STOP button and took out the sopping, heavy clothes and put them in the laundry sink. With a major effort he held back his temper. Then he stopped holding it and let out a few choice words, none of which were possible names for a band.

By the time he reentered the kitchen, it was a bustle

of activity. Dad had appeared and was mixing the ingredients for flapjacks. He was wearing a cap with the name of a photographic studio, Focus, printed on it.

Focus.

Solly looked around. Everyone in the Henson household was focused, all right. Mom was focused on her slow old jazz tune; the seven-year-old had drifted from his peas to drawing mustaches on every face in the morning newspaper; and D'Arcy had abandoned her egg temporarily and was reading a novel. She read novels the way most people eat nuts; they were littered all over the house. Book pollution.

Dad had turned on the news but was talking over it about the painting he was doing. Solly wasn't exactly sure who he was talking to. His father got up every morning at five to paint. He had turned the garage into a studio. He was wearing his black grease-monkey outfit, like the kind an auto mechanic wears, except in his case the smears and stains were cadmium yellow, crimson lake, and cerulean blue. There were more stains than usual, Solly noticed.

"Did you get any paint on the canvas?" he asked.

His father looked down admiringly at his clothes. "I've started painting in the dark," he said. "Remember that power failure? Ever since then. This way it's all *feel*. I'm not influenced by what the palette says to me."

His father always talked like that. Solly tried to imagine a talking palette with crimson lips and cerulean blue eyes.

"Why couldn't you just be interested in fishing or bowling or something?" said Solly.

"It could be worse," said Mrs. Henson from the living room. "There's a play called *You Can't Take It with You*, where the father's hobby is making fireworks in the basement. Just be thankful."

"Hey," said Mr. Henson, flipping some flapjacks onto a plate. "Why don't you call your band *Painting in the Dark*?"

"We've already got a name." The doorbell rang. Solly went to answer it. *"Madhouse,"* he said. "Guess who thought of it?"

He opened the door. It didn't matter that he was in his pajamas, it would only be Boz.

"Who is it?" called his mother.

"The crew from 'MTV,' " Solly called back as Boz entered. "They've come to film a typical morning in the life of the bass player for *Madhouse*."

"Good," said his mother. "I'll be discovered at last!"

"What's happening?" said Boz.

"The usual," said Solly. That's when he noticed that Boz had a suitcase with him. A large one.

"Can I put this in your room?" he asked.

Before Solly could answer, the phone rang.

"I'll get it," Solly's mother said. But she was still working out on the guitar—"Someone's Rockin' My Dreamboat." She'd been working on it for weeks. The phone rang and rang. The seven-year-old kept drawing, D'Arcy kept on reading, and Solly's father seemed to be writing down something he had heard on the radio.

"Amazing," said Boz, blinking a couple of times. Then he picked up his suitcase and jogged upstairs. It was left to Solly to answer the phone. But he had taken so long getting to it, he had to wait while their answering machine finished its message.

"Hi. You're talking to the disembodied voice of Barnett Henson. None of the Hensons can come to the phone right now. We're having a séance. We're trying to contact Thomas Edison beyond the grave to see if he's got any more bright ideas. But please leave a message and we'll be in touch. . . ."

"Hello?"

It was Boz's mother. She was at the office. She was phoning about Boz.

"Yes, he's here," said Solly.

She sighed with relief. They'd had a quarrel. She was just checking to see whether he was okay. Solly didn't say anything about the suitcase. "Seems okay to me," he said.

She wanted to speak to Boz, who was coming down the stairs. Solly held up the phone for him but Boz shook his head.

"He's in the bathroom, Mrs. Crosby," said Solly. "And then we're really going to have to get moving; it's kind of late. Maybe he can phone you at lunch . . . okay? Bye."

Solly hung up. Boz joined him in the hall. "Thanks," he said.

"Must have been a doozer of a fight," Solly whispered. "What'd you do?"

Boz looked like he didn't want to discuss it. He also knew he owed Solly some kind of explanation.

"My mom looked in my bankbook this morning and saw that I took out three hundred dollars of my savings. I told her I was buying a new amp."

"You bought a new amp last spring."

"That's what she said."

"So?" said Solly. "Why'd you take the money out?"

Boz got all stiff-looking. "Tell you later," he said. Then he shuffled quickly into the dining room before Solly could grill him any more.

"Look at this," said the seven-year-old, holding up the front page of the newspaper. The prime minister now sported a bright red hairdo. He also had a bad outbreak of multicolored pimples and a couple of nose rings.

"Excellent," said Boz, giving the seven-year-old a high-five. "Who's my main man?"

"Me," said the seven-year-old as their palms smacked together.

"Just in time for some flapjacks," said Mr. Henson.

"Boz, is that you?" called Mrs. Henson. "How do I make an F-sharp minor?"

Boz took the flapjacks. "It's just an F minor moved up one fret," he called, his mouth already full.

"Dad," said the seven-year-old. "Can you make me a flapjack that looks like the prime minister?"

Solly looked at the clock. "Does anybody in this house know it's eight-thirty?" Nobody answered. Solly raised his voice a couple of notches. "Does anybody care?"

The seven-year-old looked up from his drawing. "When does 'Inspector Gadget' start?" he asked.

"Fine!" said Solly. "Don't mind me."

Just then the buzzer on the washer went. He stomped through the kitchen to the laundry room, pulling the door soundly shut behind him. His wash was embroidered with torn shreds of Kleenex. Solly picked off the Kleenex and flicked it into the tub onto Earl's wet stuff.

"Serves him right," he muttered. Then he hurled each item of his own wet clothing into the dryer with a resounding boom. Underwear-*boom*-sweatshirt-*boom*-jeans-*boom*. School wasn't far. There was still a chance he could make it. With or without Boz.

He could hear the family laughing. He punched the REGULAR button on the dryer. "Maybe if I put my whole family in this dryer, they'll come out regular," he growled to himself.

Under the comforting *thut-ata-thump*, *thut-ata-thump* of the clothes cycling in their hot orbit, he stared out the laundry-room window at the bird feeder: the house finches pecking at the chickadees; the blue jays pecking at the finches; the evening grosbeaks pecking at the blue jays. Suddenly a fat black squirrel made the perilous leap from the tree trunk out to the feeder and all the birds fled into the low branches of the trees. The interloper stuffed his fat black cheeks. He looked pretty pleased with himself.

Solly flung open the back door and yelled at the squirrel, which tore down off the bird feeder and scampered back up its tree. Then Solly wondered why he'd yelled—squirrels had to eat, too.

He reentered the Madhouse. Boz, D'Arcy and the seven-year-old were clearing the dining-room table. Dad was pouring cups of tea for everyone, and every cup was different. Solly noticed that. He remembered a meal at Boz's house. Every dish, cup and plate on the table had the same pattern. There was real silverware and little stands to rest your knife on when you weren't using it and little blue glass bowls filled with salt and tiny silver spoons for the salt.

"Sounds boring," D'Arcy had said when he'd described it.

Now Solly watched his own mother, carrying what looked like a game box, join the others in the dining room. She plumped it down in the middle of the table.

"Has everybody gone out of their minds?" said Solly. He said it loudly enough that they all stopped what they were doing and looked his way.

"Want to help with the puzzle?" said Mom.

"Actually," said Solly, "I was thinking maybe I might go to school. You know—higher education? Just in case I wanted to get a real job when I grow up. Crazy idea, eh? School."

The others looked at each other with perplexed expressions on their faces.

"On a Saturday?" said D'Arcy.

The puzzle was the weirdest thing Solly had ever seen. There was no picture at all. It was completely white. Five hundred pieces and no clues. Solly wondered where his mom found such things.

Mom poured the contents of the box out on the table.

"Where do we start?" said Boz.

"I'll do the sky," said D'Arcy. "Just kidding."

They all stood around staring down at the pile of tiny white puzzle pieces. All except for the seven-year-old, who took one look and went upstairs to watch TV.

Then Mom found a corner and Boz found another corner and D'Arcy started picking out the edges. Solly's eyes would not focus at all anymore. It wasn't just the puzzle. He felt somehow as if he had been betrayed, bamboozled.

"Wait for me," he called after the seven-year-old, and went to watch "Inspector Gadget."

Inspector Gadget ran off the end of a cliff, some black-hat villain in hot pursuit. The inspector pushed a button on his wristwatch and a helicopter blade popped out of his hat. The villain sailed past him and smashed through the roof of the county jail. He landed right in his old cell. Inspector Gadget waved at him through the cell window as he fluttered by.

"That'd be great, eh?" said the seven-year-old.

"Sure," said Solly. "A few months in solitary confinement would be refreshing."

Everyone had laughed at him. Even Boz. He wanted to explain about his mistake, about thinking it was Friday morning. It was because the band usually got together on Thursday night; it was because his dad didn't usually cook breakfast on weekends; it was because Boz arrived so early—earlier than usual for a Saturday; it was because Boz's mom phoned from the office. She was in real estate and worked pretty well every day and a lot of nights, too. But still—it was an easy mistake to make, wasn't it? And how was he supposed to know his dad was up early because he had an appointment? As far as Solly could tell, his father's workdays were like the cups in the cupboard—no two alike.

A herd of commercials crossed the television screen. Downstairs the huge grandfather clock in the hall bonged out the hour. There was something wrong with it. It was on time but the song was bonkers. It was supposed to sound like St. Paul's Cathedral in London, but it sounded more like something from a cartoon. The Hensons couldn't afford to get it fixed, but it was a family heirloom—you couldn't just dump it. Most of the time Solly didn't even notice it. Today he noticed every agonizing note.

It was about then that Earl woke up and came to join the boys in front of the TV. Earl was their uncle, Mom's older brother who lived with them. He was developmentally challenged.

"Garfield," said Earl.

"You're just in time," said the seven-year-old, pushing some books and Legos onto the floor to make room on the couch. Earl sat down between them, smiling, hugging them both. Then he stood up again, as if he had sat on something sharp.

"What is it?" said Solly, smoothing the couch with his hand, looking for whatever it was that had launched Earl out of his seat. But there was nothing there, and when Solly looked up, he could see Earl trying to think of something. Earl worked pretty hard at thinking. It seemed to take over his whole big body. Then his face lit up.

"Boz," he said.

"Yep," said Solly. "Boz is here. You want to see Boz?"

"Father," said Earl.

"Father's here, too," said Solly. Earl called Mr. Henson father, even though they were really brothers-in-law.

"No," said Earl. He did some more thinking. Then he squeezed out the result of his mental effort as if he were squeezing out the last bit of toothpaste from a badly crumpled tube. "Boz's father," he said.

"Sit down," Solly said, trying to sound affectionate, patting the sofa again and pulling on Earl's pajama sleeve. "You're blocking the screen."

"Mr. Crosby," said Earl in a satisfied way. He wouldn't budge.

"Look, Garfield is going to eat a giant lasagna," said Solly impatiently.

Earl pulled his sleeve out of Solly's grasp. "Mr. Crosby," he said, more excitedly now. "Home."

"Boz doesn't have a father," said Solly.

"Sure," said Earl, smiling as if Solly had made a joke.

"Hey, look! Odie's asleep in the lasagna."

But Earl, as much as he liked Garfield, could not be deflected from his thought now that he had a good solid grip on it. Whatever he had on his mind had taken on urgent proportions.

"Come," he said. He took hold of Solly's hand. "Come and see."

Solly pulled his hand free. He didn't mean to be irritable with Earl. Earl was okay most of the time. Patiently, Earl picked up Solly's hand again, as if it were an object he had dropped and was determined not to lose.

"Come," he said. He spoke directly to Solly's hand this time, as if he might have better luck with it than with its owner. Reluctantly, Solly allowed himself to be dragged up and, hand in hand, he followed Earl to his room.

From Earl's window you could see right down Pickerel Lane. It was a perfect autumn morning. Earl pointed down the hill to Boz's house. It was white with a bright yellow door and a lawn that looked as if it had just come back from the dry cleaners. The driveway was empty. There was a battered, dirty brown car sitting out front on the road. It looked out of place.

"Mr. Crosby," said Earl. His mouth was right up against the glass. The window fogged up. He rubbed away the fog with a thick finger.

"Looks like a Buick to me," said Solly.

"Huh?"

"There's no one there," said Solly, starting to leave. But Earl could be extraordinarily stubborn. He grabbed Solly again.

"Mr. Crosby," he said. "Inside."

This time Solly shook himself free forcefully. "Mr. Crosby left when Boz was a baby," he said. "He hasn't even met his father."

"Me," said Earl, poking himself in the chest, a huge grin on his face. "I meet him."

Solly looked down the hill toward the Crosby house. He watched it for a whole minute. Nothing moved, nothing changed.

There was no one there. There never was in Boz's house. A regular-sized clock ticked politely on the mantel. The magazines were stacked neatly in a magazine rack. The top was on the toothpaste. A pine-tree-shaped air freshener was plugged into the wall socket. That was all. He'd been there.

"Boz's father," said Solly. "What next." Then he patted Earl on the shoulder and took his leave.

By now Garfield was tucking into a lasagna the size of a city block. The camera pulled back and the whole city, the whole planet was nothing but lasagna. The moon was a meatball. The seven-year-old filled Solly in on what he had missed. Earl came by but, to Solly's relief, headed downstairs.

It took Solly the rest of the cartoon and the beginning of a new stampede of commercials to realize something was wrong. No one had greeted Earl when he arrived downstairs. Dad hadn't got him some flapjacks. Mom hadn't explained about the puzzle they were working on and asked him to help. Mom always got Earl involved in things the family was doing. But this time no one had even noticed him.

Suddenly Solly leapt to his feet.

"Holy doodle," he cried.

"What?" said the seven-year-old.

"Earl's gone outside," said Solly, already on the stairs. "In his pajamas."

Solly raced downstairs through the front hall, out the door and down the path. He was halfway down the block himself before he realized that he, too, was tearing down Pickerel Lane in his pajamas.

He stopped in the middle of the street. Mr. Josephson, who was out washing his car, waved. Mr. Garvey, who was blowing leaves off his lawn with a noisy leaf-blowing machine, waved as well. Solly waved back, hitching up his pj's. Boz's voice followed him down the street, but Mr. Garvey's leaf-blowing machine obliterated the sense of what he was saying. Solly could guess.

Up ahead, he could see Earl already walking up the path to the Crosbys' front door in his pajamas and fluffy slippers. Solly had to get him. The pajama parade. Who cared, anyway? He had no credibility. He was one of those kids from the Madhouse, after all. He would just get Earl and take him home, and if any other neighbors out tending their lawns on this lovely fall morning said hello, he'd just say hello back. Maybe he'd say "Nice day" or something, as if chasing around the neighborhood with your uncle in pajamas was normal.

By the time he reached the Crosbys' driveway, he could see Earl waving at the bright yellow front door.

"Hi, there," said Earl to the door. He tapped on it again. "Hi, there."

Solly took the front steps in a single stride. He was just about to start pulling Earl away, softly urging him home, when he saw that Earl was not talking to the door. He was peering in the peephole, and in the peephole Solly caught a glimpse of an eye. It was no more than a glimpse, but it was enough.

He knocked on the door himself. No one answered. He tried the door. It was locked. But by then Boz had arrived and was already fishing his key out of his pocket.

The man inside the Crosby house was heading down the steps to the back door when they entered the house through the front. He stopped in his tracks. His shoulders hunched up, then slumped. He turned very slowly. He had a fat black briefcase, the kind a salesman might carry.

"Mr. Crosby," said Earl. "Remember me?"

The man frowned. "Nah," he said. "Never seen you before in my life." Then his gaze drifted over to Solly and past him to Boz.

"So we meet after all," he said.

Boz's face and neck turned bright red. "Let's get out of here."

Solly looked at Boz in disbelief. "What is going on?"

Boz shot Solly a glance full of alarm, but his gaze shifted back to the stranger and now his eyes seemed only full of hurt. "He was just coming by to borrow some money," he said. His eyes drifted down to the briefcase. "That must be what the large briefcase is for."

"Hey," said the man. "I can explain—"

"Don't bother," said Boz.

The man opened his mouth to speak, but he closed it again. He took a step backward down the stairs. He seemed even smaller now.

"Somebody say something!" said Solly, his voice cracking with intensity.

That's when Earl suggested they take Mr. Crosby home with them.

"Forget it," said Boz angrily. "Let's get out of here."

"It's your *house*!" said Solly.

"And I want everybody out!" said Boz. "Now."

He turned to go, but Earl had his own ideas. The stranger tried to pull away when Earl grabbed him by the arm. But Earl held on tight. The man slapped his hand. "Cut it out," he said. Earl just held on tighter. The man threatened Earl with his fist, but Boz yelled at him fiercely and he backed off. He was not a big man. And Earl was very stubborn. And strong.

As Earl triumphantly led the stranger out the front door, Solly tried to take the briefcase from him.

"It's mine," said the stranger, holding it close.

"We'll see about that," said Solly.

"Okay, okay," said the man, suddenly thrusting the briefcase into Solly's hands. "Keep it, keep it. Why would I want it, anyway?"

Solly opened it. It was empty.

"What'd ya expect?" said the stranger.

Solly didn't answer. He handed back the briefcase.

Boz walked on ahead, kicking at stones and swiping at leaves whipped up by the wind. Solly didn't know where to be: with Earl or with Boz. He walked somewhere between them. He had stopped worrying about anyone noticing him. His sense of what was normal had taken too much of a beating to bother fretting anymore.

Earl, meanwhile, was grinning like a fisherman with a prize catch. The fish had other ideas. He went along peacefully enough, but just after they passed the old Buick, the man suddenly shook his captor free and, before anyone could do a thing about it, he had hurled his big black briefcase into the car and revving up the engine.

Then he squealed off up Pickerel Lane, leaving a stretch of rubber half a block long. Earl waved at him as he drove off.

Boz came back, glancing grimly at Solly as he passed him on the way back to his house.

"You want me to come?" said Solly. Boz shook his head. Solly stood watching him half march, half run back down the lane and up the pathway. At the door he paused. He looked back at Solly and motioned him to come. Solly took one look up the lane. Earl was homeward bound, and Mrs. Henson was at the door waiting for him. He would be okay.

When Solly entered the Crosby house, he found Boz in the kitchen. On the table there was a pile of money. Boz was reading a note—two notes on one piece of paper. The original note was in Boz's handwriting. There was no salutation.

> *This is as much money as I've got. I can't get any more so don't ask. Mom doesn't know anything about this and I'm not going to tell her. Boz.*

Underneath it, in pencil, the intruder had added his own note.

> *I may be a failure, but I don't take my own kid's money.*

Solly stared at the note. "So it *was* your dad?"

"Great, eh?" said Boz. "Our big reunion."

Solly put his arms around Boz and held him very tightly. They stood that way for about as long as it took Mr. Garvey to finish blowing the leaves off his lawn. Then with a sort of shudder, Boz let it go.

He counted the money. He started laughing.

"What?" said Solly.

"There's twenty bucks missing," he said.

The two boys laughed so hard that the perfectly matched china in the cabinet shook and rattled as if a train were passing.

Then they locked up and walked back to Solly's place.

"He kept phoning," said Boz. "It seemed Mom was always out. I didn't know who he was. Then one night he told me. I guess I was glad to talk to him. I didn't tell Mom—it was between us. Anyway, one night he said he needed some cash—he called it 'mazuma'— I didn't even know what he was talking about. Just a loan, he said. He wondered if maybe I'd put in a good word for him with Mom. I guess that's when I realized he wasn't interested in me. He'd just been talking me up, trying to get on my good side. The next time he phoned I told him I had some money. He told me when he was coming and I said I couldn't be here. He made a big deal about how sad he was that we wouldn't get a chance to see each other but he didn't say he could come some other time. He sounded relieved."

Boz's throat seemed to close off on him. They

walked the rest of the way in friendly silence. Mrs. Henson was waiting on the front step.

"What was all that about?" she said.

"It's kind of hard to explain," said Boz.

"Let me try and guess," said Mrs. Henson. "I have a funny feeling that when the police check the license-plate number I wrote down, they'll find it belongs to Cecil Crosby. Am I close?"

"Don't call the cops," said Boz.

"Convince me," said Mrs. Henson.

"Don't you think this is none of our business?" said Solly.

"Convince me," said his mother. He hated it when she got in her convince-me mode. It meant she was serious. He could tell she was serious. She'd made a whole pot of coffee and there was no one there to drink it but herself. Dad had gone into town. Couldn't she see Boz was hurting?

"The guy's a goof," said Boz. "He won't come back."

"Convince me."

"There's nothing to steal, anyway."

"He broke into your home, Boz!"

"Yeah," said Boz, "home."

They were sitting at the island counter. Solly fiddled with the seven-year-old's markers, not wanting to look up. Not wanting to hear this, the hurt in Boz's voice. The anger. Solly hunkered down over the newspaper. He gave the prime minister a sprinkling of turquoise freckles, another nose ring. He was dimly aware of D'Arcy and Earl at the dining-room table, Earl humming lightly to himself, D'Arcy listening hard, but not to Earl.

Mrs. Henson said nothing. Boz struggled with the silence.

"If the cops come then Mom will find out."

"And you don't think she can handle it?"

"She's so . . . she's got a lot to do."

Mrs. Henson poured herself a cup of coffee. "I don't know Becka all that well, but she's a pretty resourceful lady."

More silence. Boz sat like a sack on the stool next to Solly. Something drifted down from the TV. "Dennis the Menace."

"I'll tell my mother," said Boz quietly. Mrs. Henson gave his shoulder a squeeze. Then she handed him the phone.

"Now?"

"Mom!" said Solly, covering his face. "Leave the poor guy alone."

"She's at work," said Boz. "She's probably out with a client."

"Then it's lucky she has a cellular phone," said Mrs. Henson.

Boz still hesitated.

"It may not be the home you want it to be, Boz, but it's *home*."

Solly looked up. His mother talked about home as though it were something sacred. Under her spell, Boz made the call. He didn't say much. What had happened, where he was. When he hung up, he looked surprised.

"She's coming right over," he said.

"Of course she is," said Mrs. Henson. "She's your mother."

Then suddenly D'Arcy said, "Oh!" very loudly.

She was staring dumbfounded at the white puzzle on the table. The others went to look.

It was finished.

Earl had finished it.

"Amazing," said Boz.

Earl grinned. "Easy," he said. "No picture to get in the way."

Becka Crosby kept her word. She came right over. She seemed quite shaken. Boz tried to console her.

"I took care of everything," he said.

And so he had. He had loaded up all the silverware and her jewelry—everything precious they owned. That's what was in the suitcase he had arrived with that morning. And that's what he had meant about there being nothing in his own house worth stealing.

"I wrapped everything really carefully." Boz showed her, misunderstanding the look of concern in her eyes.

But Becka, it seemed, wasn't all that worried about the jewelry and silverware. She just stared at Boz with wonderment. That was the word Mrs. Henson used later, when the Henson family was talking about the event among themselves. Wonderment.

After checking things over at their own house, Boz and his mother returned to the Madhouse for dinner.

Barnett Henson made it home for the celebration. Actually, he had never left. His appointment had been canceled so he had been working on his painting in the garage all day and nobody even knew. Solly watched Becka Crosby to see what she thought of this grown man in a black grease-monkey suit covered with bright splotches of paint. A man who painted in the dark. She shook his hand. Asked to see his work.

And Solly watched Becka Crosby closely over dinner, but she didn't seem to notice that none of the china matched. Didn't seem to care.

He tried to stop her from helping to clear the dishes after dinner, but she seemed to be enjoying herself.

And it was on the way back to the table for the last handful of odd cups that Becka Crosby found a lone brown egg in the flowerpot on the dining-room windowsill.

"The Easter bunny a little late this year?" she asked, holding it up.

D'Arcy grinned. "I was wondering where I left that," she said. She took it from Mrs. Crosby and was about to return it to the refrigerator when Solly stopped her.

"It's still the equinox," he said. "May I?" He took the egg from her and placed it carefully on its end on the dining-room table. Ever so slowly he took his fingers away. And it stood there, fixed in their gaze.

⊜ The Book of Changes

The big fall unit in Ms. Fidelio's class was China.

Helen kicked things off by making *chai chow fan* in the family center. She brought a wok from her parents' restaurant. It was about the size of a satellite dish. Then everybody, each with a little Chinese bowl of the stuff, sat around working on their chopsticks and saying *chai chow fan* a lot, as in: "How are you today?" "Oh, *chai chow fan*, thank you," and "What the *chai chow fan*'s the matter with you?" The family center had never smelled so gingery.

Taylor made a model of the Great Wall of China — all fifteen hundred miles of it—out of papier-mâché. On the north side of the wall he had plastic Indians on horseback attacking the wall with bows and arrows and tomahawks. He had to use Indians because he didn't have any Mongol warriors.

Amelia asked Ms. Fidelio whether this was racist, so they had to have a bit of a discussion. Taylor said the Mongols were excellent horsemen like the Indians of the North American plains, so he thought it was a pretty good substitution. Amelia thought he should call the Indians natives. Ms. Fidelio agreed and suggested he find a picture of a Mongol horseman to show the class, just for the record. Then Amelia wondered out loud whether Taylor should say "horse persons," so Ms. Fidelio suggested she write an essay on the subject. Just so they could get on with things.

Taylor also made a section of the Great Wall out of Legos.

"If you were in outer space the only *person*-made thing you would be able to see would be the Great Wall of China," he told the class. Everybody in the class imagined right then a wall of Legos you could see from outer space: red, yellow, blue and white.

On the third day of presentations, Ms. Julia Peach walked to the front of class wearing an impressive green jacket with a mandarin collar and golden dragons crawling all over it. She carried a plain-brown-paper grocery bag. Everybody sat a little higher in their seats. You never knew what The Peach was going to do next, but whatever it was, she would have practiced it first.

First she wrote I CHING on the chalkboard.

"You left out the T," said Tobias, scratching and making monkey noises. Peach rolled her eyes. She placed the bag on the front desk and from it drew a fat book with a gray cover and *I ching* written in yellow type. She held it up high in one hand like a preacher or a salesman at the fair.

"The *ee tshing*," she said. "Or, as it is sometimes called, *The Book of Changes*." She waited for complete silence. Then she began.

"*The Book of Changes* is viewed by some people as one of the great treasures of Chinese literature, first set down in the dawn of history and enlarged and edited by none other than the great philosopher Confucius five hundred years before the birth of Christ."

She said the whole sentence in a single breath.

"But it is viewed by others," she continued, "as nothing but superstition and murk." With a steely gaze she dared anyone in the room to think of the book in her hand as murk.

"*The Book of Changes* is a fortune-telling manual. And more. It is a meta-phy-si-cal account of how nature works."

By now, everyone was sucked in. There wasn't one kid in the class who knew what the word *metaphysical* meant, but it sounded right, and that was enough for the time being. Peach sounded as grand as the Great Oz. Not even Amelia would have dared to interrupt.

Slowly, Peach lowered the book to the desk. Then, like a magician, she reached into her brown paper bag again. She took out a square piece of black cloth, and, exactly like a magician, she showed the class both sides of it before laying it down on the desk. She rolled up the sleeves of her jacket. There was nothing hidden there.

"*The Book of Changes* is an oracle, a prophecy of what is to be," she said, smoothing out the cloth. "But if we are to consult the oracle, to ask it what the future holds, first we must prepare." She reached into the bag once more. Everyone expected at least a rabbit. No one expected pick-up sticks. She held them up for all to see. "Imagine these are yarrow roots."

"Arrow roots?" said Tobias. "Baby cookies?"

"*Yarrow* roots," said Peach. She rolled her eyes again. "The roots of the wildflower, yarrow."

"Oh," said Tobias, as if it all made sense now.

"I have fifty yarrow roots here," she said, holding up the pick-up sticks. She took one from the bundle in her hand and laid it aside. "This one plays no further part in the proceedings."

Everyone looked at the one blue pick-up stick laid aside on the black cloth—some a little sadly, as if it had never really had a chance. But Peach didn't let them dwell on it.

"I will now divide the remaining yarrow roots at random into two piles. From the right-hand pile I will take one yarrow root and place it between the ring finger and baby finger of my left hand." She did this. "Then, with my left hand, I will pick up the left-hand heap and pick from it with my right hand bundles of four until there are four or fewer left over."

Everyone was glued to what Peach was doing with the pick-up sticks. But no matter how smart she was or how hard she had practiced, large hands and agile fingers were not among her many gifts. Soon there were pick-up sticks sticking out every which way from her hand as if she'd been wrestling a porcupine. Pick-up sticks were falling on the table and clattering on the floor and generally making the telling of the future very difficult.

At the first noisy smirk from the crowd, Peach dropped the whole lot on the black cloth and dusted her hands as if glad to be rid of them. It was glorious.

The only thing better than a real magician is a comic magician.

She wrapped up the pick-up sticks in the black cloth and put the whole thing back in the bag.

"Luckily, the yarrow-root method is not the only way to consult the oracle." From her pocket she drew three coins. She came out from behind the desk and showed them to her classmates, who crowded around. The coins were bronze—Chinese coins with a hole in the center and, as Peach pointed out, an inscription on one side only.

"Ordinary pennies will do," she said, but she said it in such a way that you wouldn't be caught dead consulting the oracle with anything but bronze.

Reverently, she collected up *The Book of Changes*.

"By throwing the three coins, you determine which of the prophecies in this book foretells *your* future." She closed her fist around the three coins and raised it in the air. She was holding the book up, too. Now she looked like a priest and a salesman and a prizefighter. Somebody did a drum roll on his desk top.

"Is there anyone in the class fearless enough to gaze into the ancient *Book of Changes* to see what lies ahead?"

Everyone, even Ms. Fidelio, wanted nothing better. Peach held a finger up to her lips for silence. "This is not like reading your horoscope in the paper," she warned them. "You must have a question ready to ask the oracle."

Everyone quickly started thinking up questions.

"Am I going to find a thousand-dollar bill on the way home today?"

"Will the Oilers ever make it to the Stanley Cup again?"

"Will Mark Paul ask me out?"

The questions poured in, but Peach shook her head sadly, as if each one was slightly more pathetic than the last and some of them beneath contempt. Then Tobias, sitting quietly, watching with admiration, stuck up his hand. Peach called out his name, and he stood.

"I haven't done my Chinese project," he said.

"That's not a question," said Peach.

"I have no idea what to do for my Chinese project."

Peach tapped her foot. "Toby," she said, "the oracle is getting impatient."

"Okay, okay. I have a question," he said. "I want to ask *The Book of Changes* what to do for my assignment."

Peach was caught off guard. She looked at Ms. Fidelio. Everyone looked at Ms. Fidelio. Ms. Fidelio consulted her notebook.

"I thought you were doing Popular Chinese Games and Pastimes," she said.

"I was," said Tobias. "But it wasn't challenging enough." He didn't bother to mention that he hadn't done a thing on it yet.

Ms. Fidelio leaned her elbows on her desk and leaned her chin on her knuckles. "Well, this will certainly be a challenge," she said. "You're due to speak to the class tomorrow."

"Let him do it, let him do it," yelled the class.

All except Amelia. "I don't think it's fair if people change their topic," she said. Everyone groaned and said rude things and told her to get back to writing her paper on "horse-persons."

Then Helen offered a suggestion. "My father reads the *I ching*," she said. "It's all about taking chances."

"Right," said Peach.

"How so?" asked Ms. Fidelio. Helen shrugged. Peach thought about it. Mostly she found herself thinking that she had never had a teacher as lovely and clever as Ms. Fidelio. If she had thought more about the fate of her good friend Tobias, she might not have spoken with such zeal.

"When you seriously ask the *I ching* a question, you are allowing chance to enter into your dull and dreary life," Peach said.

That was it. Tobias was convinced. So was Ms. Fidelio. "Well, why not," she said.

The class cheered.

So Tobias was summoned to the front and, with Peach as his guide, threw the coins six times. Peach added up the score of each throw. The inscribed side was worth two, the other side three. She checked the instructions in the back of the book. Then she wrote on the board six lines—a hexagram:

She consulted the key in *The Book of Changes* and turned to hexagram number thirty-five. It had a name,

Chin, which meant Progress. But time had pro-
gressed, and there wasn't any left to read it to the
class right then.

"Good start, Toby," said Ms. Fidelio. "Now let's see
you make some real progress on that assignment of
yours."

Her own assignment over, Peach loaned Tobias *The
Book of Changes*. She loaned him her coins, too. For
good luck.

He read the oracle very carefully. It sure didn't say
anything like "You must steal from its lair the baby
teeth of a dragon," which was the kind of thing some
of the class were hoping for. And it didn't say, "You
will go on a long ocean voyage with a tall dark
stranger," which was the kind of thing a bunch of
other kids had expected. Frankly, it didn't seem to
give Tobias a whole lot of direction.

He read the oracle again out loud walking home
with Peach. She interrupted him every now and then
when it looked like he was going to walk into a tele-
phone pole, or there was a car turning in front of him.

"Let it *talk* to you," she said.

He held the book up to his ear. "Hello? Hello? Anyone there?"

"Toby," said Peach, with as much patience as she
could muster. "When this book was written, there
were no phones. There weren't even any schools."

"I wish," said Tobias.

They walked along a bit in silence.

"You could always do your original project on mah-jong and Chinese checkers."

Tobias shook his head. "No, I can't." He sighed.

"Why not?"

"Because," he said, stabbing the cover of the *I ching*, "I let you convince me to let chance enter into my dull and dreary life."

The Book of Changes. No wonder he'd fallen for it. Such a wonderful name for a book. But even when Tobias had read hexagram thirty-five at home for the third time, it didn't do much for him. Didn't give him much of an idea for a project.

He tried saying the three-page oracle out loud, as if it were a magic spell. It made a great-sounding spell, especially if he only used the juicy bits.

"Progress. The light rising from the earth . . . clarity . . . the powerful prince is honored with horses in large numbers . . . wise ruler, he rewards his loyal subjects fittingly. . . ."

It sounded like the voice-over for a TV commercial. But what did it all mean?

Still, the book itself seemed kind of magical. If this were a movie, Tobias thought, he would lay it on his bedside table and as soon as he fell asleep the book would start to light up—pulsing hot—and throb like an alien heart. He would wake up in a sweat and there would be a genie—a Chinese one with long curled fingernails and a parrot on his shoulder.

Or he would wake up to the smell of incense and

the top of the book would creak open and there would be a staircase down into an adventure of one kind or another. He would be transformed, of course—made smaller—so as to journey into the book. There would be dragons and Mongol hordes and lots of *chai chow fan* in case he got hungry.

But by eight o'clock nothing like that had happened, and Tobias began to get frantic. His mind began grasping at straws. Maybe he could do a little play? The hexagram represented the sun rising over the earth. He could cut out a sun and staple it onto a stick and show it rising in the sky while he quoted stuff from the book. He remembered Peach's green jacket with the dragon on it. He could dress up like a feudal lord; he'd seen a picture of one somewhere. He tried out a line or two in front of the mirror in the bathroom, wearing a wicker basket on his head while he waved a crayon sun around, shedding clarity across the land. He felt like Bert on "Sesame Street" stuck in one of Ernie's school recitals. The class would go crazy. He'd be laughed out of town.

He tried writing a rock song on the guitar.

> *The sun in the morning shines brighter than*
>   *anything.*
> *The prince who is smart doesn't mess with*
>   *the king.*
> *Oh, oh, the clinging fire.*
> *Oh, oh, rising higher and higher.*

He snapped a D-string. It was a sign.

"To be conscious of danger brings good fortune.

No blame," he read in one of the commentaries accompanying hexagram thirty-five.

Maybe he could tell Ms. Fidelio he'd made a big mistake and she'd let him do the pastimes and recreations project some other time. But, no—even as he thought about it, he knew he couldn't go back.

"Progress. The light rising from the earth . . . clarity . . . the powerful prince is honored with horses in large numbers . . . wise ruler, he rewards his loyal subjects fittingly. . . ."

He tried his incantation again, this time jingling the three Chinese coins in his hand. Nothing.

Maybe it was this hexagram that was the problem. As far as prophecies went, it seemed pretty boring. Then Tobias realized that only Peach knew which hexagram he had "chosen," and she wouldn't rat on him. So he checked out some of the other oracles. There were sixty-four in all. He threw the coins a bunch of times, adding up the values the way Peach had shown him and coming up with new hexagrams. Then he gave up on the coins altogether and just thumbed through the book to see if there was a hexagram with his name written on it. Nothing.

Peach phoned to see how he and the *I ching* were doing.

"We're not talking," he said.

"Maybe you're expecting too much?"

"I'm expecting a project," he said. "And so is Ms. Fidelio. The trouble is you made it sound so fantastic when you were doing your presentation, I was sure I'd open the book and it would be there—my project, all written up neatly on lined paper with an A+ at the top."

There was a pause while Peach tried to figure out if he was blaming her or giving her a compliment.

"It's all my fault," said Peach. "I made it sound like a game and it's not."

"No," said Toby. "I kind of figured that out."

Then they said good-bye and hung up.

The phone rang again almost right away. It was Peach.

"To one person its spirit appears as clear as day; to another, shadowy as twilight; to a third, dark as night."

"What does?" said Toby.

"The Book of Changes."

Peach sounded pretty excited. Toby tried to figure out why. "Did you make that up?"

"Nope," said Peach. "It was in the book somewhere. I had it in my notes. Thought it might be helpful."

"Oh," said Tobias. "Thanks."

"Think nothing of it," said Peach, and hung up for good.

Tobias repeated to himself what Peach had told him. "To one person its spirit appears as clear as day; to another, shadowy as twilight; to a third, dark as night.

"Well, that solves everything," he said.

By nine-thirty, sweaty, brain-wringing desperation had given way to gloom. By ten, gloom had given way to idle doodling, a sure sign that total exhaustion and defeat were just around the corner. It was all over. He was going to get a Z on the biggest project of the fall unit. Tobias closed the great treasure of Chinese literature with a thump and went down to join his folks in front of the TV.

"Finished your project?" his mom asked.

"No," said Tobias. "It finished me."

He woke up in the dark. He looked at *The Book of Changes* where he'd left it on his bedside table, just in case. It was not glowing magically from within. But when his eyes could focus better, he saw that there was enough glow to read the title. The moon was full. Its light fell across the book.

Tobias slithered farther down into bed, and the light of the moon fell across his face. He closed his eyes and imagined a moon tan. He was filled with tranquillity, a peacefulness that he couldn't understand and that did not seem deserved, all things considered.

He looked at his alarm; it was 3:00 A.M.

What had he been thinking? Something Peach had said. It's not a game. That was it. But why wasn't it?

Toby sat up a bit and folded his hands under his head. He had been going to do his project on games in the first place. Why couldn't his prophecy, hexagram thirty-five, become a game?

"What do you think, Moon?" he asked.

The Moon said, "Hey, when you've been around a few billion years, even the Great Wall of China looks like a game."

Yes.

Tobias sat up a little bit more, not ready yet to let

go of the warmth of his bed. He felt good somehow, and he couldn't think why. He had no project and it was due that very day. But lying there in the absolute quietness of his moonlit room, it hardly mattered.

"It's all just a game," he said to himself.

Yes.

He didn't jump out of bed. He slid out silently. He turned on his desk lamp. He hated what it did to his eyes, to the softness of the moonlight, but he had work to do. No—that wasn't it. He had a game to play.

He dug out his Monopoly game from the shelf in his closet and dumped the contents on the floor. At his desk he re-covered the box in red construction paper. It was a very Chinese kind of red. When the box was completely covered, it already looked good. But his mind was waking up now. The yin-yang symbol: Cindy had done a project on that. It was all about the negative and positive principles of the universe, all in balance. It was a great-looking symbol; he had doodled it all over his notebooks. Now it seemed as if he had just been practicing for this.

With white and black construction paper he made the yin-yang symbol and glued it onto his mysterious-looking red box. The calm in him guided his scissors. His circle came out very circular, considering it was three in the morning.

It was as he was holding up the box cover at arm's length, admiring it, that the wise and powerful Chinese warlord came into the room, probably down moon steps from the sky. Tobias didn't really hear him enter.

"Nice box," said the warlord, taking off his helmet. He stretched and sprawled on Tobias's bed. "Is it a game? I like games."

"It's actually just a box, so far," said Tobias. "I haven't thought of what goes in it."

The warrior nodded. "Perseverance brings good fortune," he said.

Right. Tobias looked at the Monopoly board. He had a couple of hours—three, max—to make up a game. It probably took the Monopoly people three years to think up a game. Luckily the warlord from the moon, who seemed to know *The Book of Changes* by heart, could also read his mind.

"Tobias," he said, "if one meets with no confidence, one should remain calm."

Calm. That was how he had felt when he first woke up. Unruffled. If he panicked now, all he would have to show for tonight would be an empty red box.

"Any other good suggestions?" he asked the prince.

The prince was playing with Tobias's alarm clock. "One obtains great happiness from one's ancestress," he said.

"Of course," said Tobias. "Why didn't I think of that?"

He was joking, but then it occurred to him that the only ancestress he knew, his grandmother Soyko, had given him a subscription to *National Geographic*. There had been an issue a few months back on China.

"Thanks," he said.

"Everything serves to further," said the prince.

"Hold that thought," said Tobias. The *National Geographic*s were downstairs in the living-room bookcase.

"Bring me back some cranberry juice," said the prince. "I'm parched."

Tobias brought back a whole jug of cranberry juice and a bowl of nacho chips. Fighting Mongol hordes was probably grueling work.

But he didn't have time to chat about it. He had things to do.

First of all, he covered the Monopoly board with a collage of Chinese landscapes: the Yangtze River by moonlight, mists of morning over a rice paddy, bamboo jungles, fairy-tale mountains. It was through this landscape that the players would find their way. But to where?

"All journeys proceed toward the center," said the prince.

"Good one," said Tobias. His path would spiral from the edge of the board in toward the center. And then what? He looked over at the prince, who was lying on the bed looking cockeyed at a poster of Axl Rose on the ceiling. Rose, his long hair flying, was wearing a kilt and screaming into a microphone.

"Reminds me of Wen Ch'ang, the way he handles that scepter," said the prince. "He lived through seventeen successive lives before being invested by the August Personage of Jade with the function of Grand Emperor of Literature."

"Oh," said Tobias. "How do you suppose I should end my game?"

The prince thought for a moment. "The weak progresses and goes upward," he said.

Upward. Tobias riffled through the cut-up *National Geographic*. Ah-ha! At the end of the quest, right in the middle of the board, an ancient cloud-enshrouded castle.

The prince hopped off the bed and came over to the desk. He stroked his chin. He nodded approvingly. "And how will you mark your path?" he said.

Tobias knew immediately: the self-adhesive labels his mother used for stuff she put in the freezer.

"Bring back some more of those chips," said the prince.

"Shhhh," said Tobias. But he brought back the whole bag.

When he returned, the prince had been messing about in Tobias's closet and had found his baseball bat. He was swinging it around like some piece of weaponry. Tobias would have to explain baseball to him. And rock 'n' roll. Some other time.

The freezer labels were yellow. The prince liked that. He stuck a few on the breastplate of his armor.

"For a prince, you sure like horsing around," said Tobias.

"Thus," said the prince, "the superior man himself brightens his bright virtue."

How many steps from beginning to end? Sixty-four: the number of hexagrams in *The Book of Changes*.

Tobias's mind was alert now, no longer distracted by the antics of the prince from the moon. He was unruffled and purring.

There would have to be chance cards. The *I ching* was all about chance. The contestant would throw the coins and add up the result. If you got three threes, you moved nine spaces but you had to turn up a Yin chance card. If you got three twos, you turned up a Yang chance card. Perfect. And all the chance cards would slow you down because otherwise the game would be over way too quickly.

Tobias took his chances from *The Book of Changes*.

> *The wind is too strong for the traveler. It blows you back four steps.*
> *You have misplaced your magic tortoise. Go look for him on step number six.*
> *The hamster is stuck on his wheel. Miss a turn.*
> *The alarmed citizens throw stones at you. Start over.*

There were six Yin chances and nine Yang. It all made sense. He pasted the penalties onto cards taken from matching decks of playing cards—blue and red—which already had very oriental-looking designs on the back.

Tobias had borrowed a game of mahjong from his great-aunt Sophia when he had been going to do the project on popular Chinese games and pastimes. So now, for counters in his own invented game, he decided to use the little blocks that had the symbols of the four winds on them.

The prince came over and looked at the game of mahjong.

"Very fancy," he said.

It was. And it almost undid Tobias.

The mahjong game came housed in a beautiful hinged box with dovetailed joints. Looking at the many pieces inside, Tobias suddenly became downhearted. It was very old, and the tiles were delicately carved out of yellowing ivory with pictures of herons and bamboo stalks. It was far more complicated and beautiful than his own game cut from construction paper and magazines.

Suddenly he was overcome with tiredness. It was 6:00 A.M. With his last bit of energy, Tobias took the four counters from the mahjong box and placed them in his own game. He closed the lid. He switched off the light. The darkness was lighter than it had been when he had jumped out of bed all full of fire and invention three hours earlier. The sun would be up soon to obliterate the moon. It did that. But now the light was only dreary.

He lay down on his bed, drained. Three whole hours.

There wasn't much left of the prince. He was fading fast in the gathering light of day. He picked up his cumbersome helmet and placed it on his head. But before he left, he stood looking down at Tobias, smiling a princely smile.

"Progressing, but turned back," said the prince. "Solitary, he walks in the right. Composure is not a mistake. One has not yet received the command."

Then he was gone.

"Bye," said Tobias sleepily. "Thanks."

He lay for a moment feeling his limbs unknot themselves.

Then, in the dull gray light, he got up one more time and opened the lid of his game. It was pretty good, really. There was only one thing left to do. It had to have a name. So he cut out letters that were *National Geographic* yellow and pasted them on the red cover in one corner. He cut them out as carefully as he could and tried to make them look as if they might have been made with brush strokes by a Chinese calligrapher.

The name of the game was Progress.

"You big lunk," I said to Turlough, scratching him behind the ear.

"Woof," he said.

Mrs. Campion was still on the phone. Or maybe she was just politely waiting until I left so that she didn't have to disappoint me. She was just being nice about buying two subscriptions. They were always so generous about paying me for doing the lawn and other errands.

Suddenly it seemed completely crummy that these nice neighbors should be plagued by me trying to sell them stuff. I could imagine Mr. Campion at dinner. "What's he selling now, dear, a new Pontiac? Of course, we'll buy it. Clarke's such a nice kid. . . ."

I couldn't stand it. I didn't want her to buy *TV Guide* just to be nice. I went all-over cold. If she really wanted it, she would already have a subscription, a smart woman like Mrs. Campion. Why hadn't I thought of that before?

I couldn't stand the suspense any longer. I had to get out of there, I had to act quick. I pushed Turlough backward into the vestibule.

"Tell her I had to go home for lunch," I whispered to him.

"Woof," he said. Maybe "lunch" sounded like "lunk" to him.

Then I was gone. I ran down the street as fast as I could. I was already home when I realized that I had left my one and only copy of *TV Guide* with Mrs. Campion. With a kind of sad relief, I realized that my career as a door-to-door salesman was over.

My mother was at the door when I arrived.

"Mrs. Campion just phoned to apologize for being so rude," she said. "She had to talk to Mrs. Henkell-Trocken about some urgent March of Dimes business."

"She wasn't rude," I said, slumping in the chair in the hall, out of breath.

"She wants two subscriptions to *TV Guide*," said Mom. "And Mrs. Henkell-Trocken is interested, too."

"Oh, that's just great!" I said. And stomped up to my room.

Apart from the baseball mitt with Hank Aaron's signature, one of the reasons I had wanted to sell *TV Guide* was because that summer was boring. We didn't have a cottage, and my parents couldn't afford to send me to camp, and Cary and Tony and the other guys were all away. But selling was too difficult. I knew that now. For someone plagued with the What ifs, it was a minefield. It was like asking a person on crutches to cross a floor covered with banana peels. It was like asking Godzilla to sell bone china at Birks Jewelers. It was like asking a blind person to interior-decorate your home.

After lunch, I told Mom I was going to go and see Mrs. Campion, but when I hopped on my bike I rode straight over to Cary's and then to Tony's, even though I knew they were away. I was hoping maybe one of them had caught chicken pox and had been sent home. Then I'd catch chicken pox. Catching chicken pox wouldn't be so bad. Scratching would at least give me something to do.

But neither of them was there. So I rode over to the park.

It was noonday hot. I pulled to a stop in the shade of a huge chestnut tree and surveyed the grounds. There were some kids there, but no one I knew.

At one end of the park, five guys were playing weird games with a girl's bicycle. One of them was sitting in the basket on the front. I didn't think I wanted to know them.

I looked back toward the Lyon Street stairs. Mrs. Campion! She was out walking Turlough. She'd see me if I tried to make a run for it. All I could do was slink over to the bushes—there were openings and paths there—and hope she didn't notice my bike, which I left on the grass under the tree. One wheel turning.

The bushes were deep and dry and thirsty with yellow flowers. I parted the dusty leaves and trained my eye on Mrs. Campion. As soon as she passed, I planned to sneak back out and head up the Lyon Street exit. By now she probably had signed up fifty people to buy *TV Guide* from me. Anyway, I was so busy watching her progress that I didn't notice the girl sitting quietly a little bit up the hill behind me. Not until she spoke.

"Who are you hiding from, please?" she asked.

I turned. She was about seven, I guess. Her skin was chestnut brown, her hair blue-black. She wore a yellow ribbon in it and a clean yellow dress and yellow sneakers. She didn't look like she usually hung out in the bushes.

"I am sorry," she said. "I astonished you."

"It's okay," I said. But I was pretty astonished.

She smiled and slid on her backside down the hill next to me. "Is it those horrid boys who you are hiding from?" she asked.

I didn't answer right off. I was staring at the red mark on her forehead. It was perfectly round, like a bullet hole. I had never seen someone from India before, not up close. Or maybe I had, in a magazine, but never a real kid.

"Those reckless boys have stolen my bicycle," she said.

I looked out across the park through the dusty leaves and the veil of yellow flowers to where the boys were. They were standing in a wide circle playing a kind of catch with the girl's bike, shooting it back and forth to one another. They looked tough. Probably went to Glashan Elementary.

"You should get it back," I said. Luckily, the little girl didn't seem to notice what a stupid remark it was.

"I told them I was going home immediately to get my big brother who would show them a thing or two," she said.

"But he wasn't home?"

"I don't have a big brother," she said sadly. Then her eyes grew huge and she smiled. "But very soon I will have a little brother."

I looked back at the boys across the park. "How soon?" I said. I didn't think he would be much help.

"Why, this very afternoon," she said. "My mother is going into the hospital and she will come back with a baby and I am hoping—oh, I am hoping—it will be a brother. It is because of him that I have this new bicycle."

I couldn't get over it. It was a brand-new bike and she was as cheery as could be even though it had been stolen. I wished I could do something. I didn't think they would really take it away with them. Maybe they'd dump it in the fountain or something and I could help the girl fish it out. If only I could assure her that that was all that would happen.

"Perhaps you know these boys," she said. "And could ask them for my bicycle back?"

I tried to imagine it. "Hi, guys. Mind if I take this bike back? Thanks." I had a pretty good imagination, but I couldn't see it happening like that.

"You are big, too," she said hopefully. Then she looked serious again. "Well, almost big."

Maybe when they get good and bored, I thought, they'll leave it. And if they don't? Then I would ask for it. But if I did, even if they gave it to me—which I doubted—they would remember me and probably get me some other time. Or *my* bike. I would be marked for life.

"They called me a wog," she said. "Do you know, please, what that might be?"

"Shhh!" I said. Mrs. Campion and Turlough were walking nearby on the path. Turlough sniffed my bike. Mrs. Campion dragged him away. She was afraid he was going to pee on it, but he knew whose bike it was even if his master didn't.

A wog. I didn't know what it was, but it made my blood boil. My eyes wouldn't focus properly. That's

when I noticed that the big floppy yellow flowers behind which I was hiding were infested with little black
bugs.

"Turlough," said Mrs. Campion, yanking on his
leash. "You big lunk."

Turlough barked.

That's when it came to me.

"I could be your brother," I whispered.

The girl gazed at me with an amused look in her
eye. "You have yellow hair," she said.

But I was miles ahead of her. "Come on," I said. I
grabbed her hand and sprang out of the bushes, much
to Mrs. Campion's surprise.

"Why, Clarke," she said, her hand on her chest.
"You scared us, didn't he, Turlough?"

Turlough woofed the deep-in-the-throat-I'm-a-
wolf-hunting-dog kind of bark he always did. It was
great to hear.

"Can I borrow him?" I asked.

"Borrow Turlough?"

"Just for a minute," I said. Then I explained about
the guys who had stolen the girl's bike and how they'd
called her a wog. Mrs. Campion was shocked.

"And what is your name, my dear?" she said.

"Amila," said the girl, shaking Mrs. Campion's
hand.

So Mrs. Campion sat down on the nearest park
bench with Amila while I went about my plan.

Turlough and I nosed around in my bike bag. There
was my baseball mitt—my scruffy old falling-apart
mitt that I would now be stuck with for life—my
Milwaukee Braves cap and my mirror sunglasses.

Even though every kid I knew was away somewhere, I always carried my baseball stuff just in case I ran into a game. Now it seemed I was going to get a completely different kind of game.

My yellow hair was summer-short. Although the hat didn't completely cover it, it was a start. There was also my bike repair kit. I never went anywhere without it. In it was a can of oil. I "goinked" some on my fingers. That's the sound the can makes—*goink, goink, goink.*

I spread the oil on the back of my hand. My hand got brown. Not very brown, like Amila. Just a kind of smeary, oily brown. Carefully, with my eyes scrinched shut, I started applying the oil to my face and neck and arms. *Goink, goink, goink.*

I pushed Turlough away. He was trying to lick my face. I goinked some oil on his nose to keep him at bay.

"Ah!" said Amila when she saw me. "Now you really are turning into my big brother." But she was teasing me. I wasn't anywhere near as brown as she was. I just smelled funny.

"What are you doing?" asked Mrs. Campion.

"It's just a little something to hide behind," I said. "Come on, Turlough."

Holding his lead with both hands close to his thick neck, I set off. We headed across the grass to the circle of boys playing catch with Amila's new bike.

I didn't know what it would be like to be blind, but I tried to imagine it. I kept my eyes open behind my mirror glasses, but I walked as if I was being led by Turlough. And I let Turlough lead me right into the middle of the circle game. Just as one of the boys launched the bike.

"Hey, watch out!"

The bike came straight toward me. Blindly, I put out my hand, stopping it before it could hit me. It fell at my feet. One boy ran to get the bike, but with all the excitement, Turlough barked, and the boy stopped.

"You could get killed," he said.

"Oh, I'm sorry," I said, trying to imitate Amila's voice. "You astonished me." I stopped right there in the middle of the circle and blindly patted Turlough's big head with my free hand.

None of the boys came toward me.

"So get lost!" said one of them.

"Actually, I am lost," I said. "My little sister told me some boys had stolen her bicycle and I am looking for them to teach them a lesson. Could you, please, direct me to these horrid boys?"

One of them moved a little closer. "Get outa here," he said. "We'll give you to ten, 'cause you're a blind wog."

I leaned close to Turlough's ear. "Big lunk," I whispered.

"Woof," said Turlough.

The nearest boy backed up.

I hadn't known exactly what I was going to do. I just figured that with Turlough there, it really didn't matter what I did. Now it was coming to me.

"What is that, Turlough?" I said.

I leaned close again as if trying to hear something. Close enough to whisper the "L" word whenever I felt like it.

"You say these are the horrid boys? (Lunk.)"

"Woof."

"There are how many? (Lunk.)"

"Woof."

"Five? (Lunk.)"

"Woof."

"So many boys ganging up on a little girl? (Lunk.)"

"Woof."

The boys weren't holding back anymore. They were moving in. Pressing closer. I hadn't counted on that. Maybe they wanted to hear what I was whispering to the dog. Or maybe they were beginning to realize what just about everybody does a few minutes after they meet Turlough. He may be very large, but his face is so friendly, you know he couldn't hurt a fly. Not on purpose, at least.

"That dog ain't talking."

"And that kid ain't blind."

"And he ain't a wog, either. He's a fake."

I had to think quick. They were closing in, talking each other up, getting braver. I held Turlough close. He was panting away and smiling. I knew what *he* was thinking. "Oh, boy. Company."

Soon they were crowding all around me.

One of them reached out across the dog and slid a finger across my cheek. He looked at the grease, smelled it.

"What is this?" he said.

I gulped for breath. When I spoke, I dropped the fake accent.

"It's wog juice," I said. "I'm part white, part *wog*."

"Hey, Ernie, looks like you got some on you," said one of the guys. They laughed as Ernie wiped the bicycle oil off on his jeans.

"Shut up," he said, shoving one of the guys.

"Ernie's a wo-og," they chanted. "Ernie's a wo-og."

"Yuck," said one of them. "And he stinks like a wog, too."

That did it. I moved in close to the one nearest me. He backed off, maybe only because my face stank of bicycle oil.

"When the sun gets really hot, it brings out the wog in me," I yelled at his face. "And the part of me that's wog is really angry about what you did to this brand-new bicycle! Look at it."

They looked. I couldn't believe it.

I reached down, grabbed the bike by the handle and jerked it up. I was breathing hard. The basket on the front was stretched out of shape. My throat and face ached. I was afraid I was going to cry. I couldn't talk to them anymore. Couldn't look at them.

"Look at this, Turlough," I shouted. "Look what these big lunks have done."

Turlough barked. Angrily.

The boys really started backing off now. Turlough was dancing around, pulling on his leash.

"We were just playin' around," said one.

"You can have the dumb bike," said another.

"Come on, guys," said a third.

And then they were off. Like fly-hunting bats in the twilight, zigzagging every which way, they dipped and darted toward the Lyon Street exit.

Mrs. Campion and Turlough and I walked Amila and her bike home.

"That was very brave, Clarke," said Mrs. Campion.

When I told my mother about the incident in the park, she said, "And did you remember to talk to Mrs. Campion about the *TV Guide* subscription?"

I hadn't. It had completely slipped my mind. Funny how you can forget important things like *TV Guide* when you are rescuing a little girl's brand-new bike from five thugs. I didn't say that to my mom. I said something I'd heard my dad say.

"No. Some of us just aren't cut out for sales, Mom."

I guess Amila found out my address from Mrs. Campion. Anyway, that evening just before dinner, she arrived at my house. I went to the door. She was taking a cloth bundle from the wrecked basket of her bike.

"For you and your family," she said, handing it to me. The bundle was warm in my hands.

My mom came to the door and introduced herself. I opened the bundle. Fragrant steam came out as the flaps of warm, white cloth fell open.

"They are called *samosas*," Amila said. "You eat them."

I didn't know what to do, so she showed me. She ate one of the little savory packets—kind of like a semicircular egg roll. I tried one. And so did my mother. Then my father came out with his newspaper to see what all the noise was about and he tried one, too. There we all were munching *samosas*. They were very spicy.

"My auntie made them," said Amila. Then her eyes got very big. "But I have forgotten the most important news, Clarke. Now I am the proud sister of *two* brothers."

"Twins?" I said.

"No," she said. Laughing, she ran down the path to her new bicycle and, pumping hard, headed home.

"I wonder if the guys from Mary Magdalene rubbed the toe," says Joel.

"They're gonna need it," says me. Then we swagger into the arena, our feet sticking out to either side, silent now, caught up in expectation, imagining strapping on a goalie's trappings, imagining a goal-less season.

"The boy's cracking," says a woman sitting about four seats away from Joel and me. Tyler has just missed blocking a shot that, luckily, hit the goalpost. Mary Magdalene is coming on hard. The arena is about half full, which is impressive for an afternoon game.

"Have you seen her before?" Joel whispers. I shake my head and steal another glance. She's about my mom's age, but she's not anything like my mom. She's got about a ton of makeup on, and she's smoking. There is no smoking allowed in the arena, but everybody's too caught up with the game to care. Besides, she doesn't look like someone you'd want to cross. She's wearing a fur coat, and the fur still has its head on; looks like it might bite your head off if you got too close.

"Somebody'd better score on him soon or the poor kid's gonna crack," she says to no one in particular.

I look at Joel. His face is mad, but he doesn't say anything.

"Maybe she's a teacher at Mary Magdalene," I whisper. Joel cracks up.

Then Christ the King gets a penalty and Mary Magdalene puts on the pressure. They fire off a couple of fast ones from the point. Tyler handles them with ease. The crowd cheers, but it's a strained kind of sound, as if a huge fist has closed around the arena. Christ the King kills the penalty and turns the game around, taking the action back down the ice.

"Who's he think he is, God?" says the woman. She isn't talking to us, though we're the closest people to her.

"I think she's drunk," says Joel.

"I think she's wacko."

I don't think she heard us, but suddenly she turns to look our way. We just watch the game, trying not to laugh. We're waiting for her to say something to us. Then the buzzer goes and it's intermission. It's 1–0 for Christ the King. The buzzer stops, but the buzzing in the arena doesn't.

Joel and I slip out for a Coke. We get back to our seats and are sitting there talking when suddenly the woman is right behind us, leaning forward. Up close, her fur looks pretty flea-bitten.

"You think I don't know?" she says. "You think I don't know what I'm saying?"

It isn't really a question, so we don't answer.

"His old man was just the same," she says. " 'Cept Randy was playing for higher stakes."

The teams are skating onto the rink. Joel and I turn our attention to the ice surface, clean and shining after the Zamboni. We concentrate on Tyler, roughing up the surface in front of his net so he'll have more traction. The woman doesn't move. She lights another cigarette. Joel coughs. Tyler bangs his goalposts with his stick. *Bang, bang.*

"Bah, superstition," says the woman. "That ain't gonna help him." She laughs a sandpapery laugh. She blows out a long line of smoke. Joel coughs again. His asthma is getting to him.

"Do you mind," I say to her.

She looks at us as if she hadn't really noticed anyone was there. It takes her a minute to figure out what I'm saying. Then she looks at her cigarette and, dropping it to the floor, she puts it out with the pointy toe of her high-heeled boot. It's black leather but salt-stained and ratty.

"Thanks," says Joel.

"You know the Longo boy?" she asks.

We don't answer. The action has started. Tyler is at the far end of the rink now, and Mary Magdalene gets a breakaway. The player loses the puck, though, and all Tyler has to do is fall on it. Still, he jumps up screaming at the skater, who has glided too close by him.

"He's strung way out," says the woman. Then she leans forward again. "You friends of Tyler Longo?"

Joel looks sideways at me. As if.

"His name's Taylor," I say to her. She laughs.

"Tyler Taylor," she says, chuckling. "Randy woulda loved that."

I keep my eyes on the game, but my mind can't let go of what the woman said. I steal a peek at Joel. He heard it, too.

Just then, Mary Magdalene poke-checks the puck

from Christ the King and takes a ferocious slap shot from in close. Like magic, Tyler throws out his glove arm and plucks the puck out of the air. The crowd goes wild.

"He's amazing!" says Joel reverently.

"You wanna know somethin'?" says our uninvited neighbor.

I'm just about to say no when she coughs loudly—badly—and doubles up, gathering her flea-bitten coat around her as if she's trying to keep her lungs inside her skinny body. One of the creatures who make up her coat is staring at me with a flat brown stare.

"He's only human," she says finally, in a hoarse whisper.

Joel is angry. "Yeah, maybe," he says, "but he's a lot better than some humans." He doesn't turn toward her, but she knows who the comment is intended for.

I make a grimace. I'm afraid she might start kicking us with those pointy boots. But she sits there, still as can be. It's as if the combination of her coughing spree and Joel's insult has knocked the breath out of her.

I can't help it; I feel sorry for her. Once, when the action comes down to our end, I steal a glance at her again. I notice she's shivering. She's sick, I think. She doesn't look quite so scary anymore.

Then Christ the King scores again.

"You see," says Joel, turning to her as we jump up and down. "Nobody's going to beat him. Nobody."

It's a dumb thing to say, really. Tyler didn't score the goal. But I sort of know what Joel means. Christ the King has gotten its second wind and the other team is folding.

The woman smiles at Joel, almost sweetly. "Maybe not today," she says, calmly now. "But, for his sake, I hope soon."

Our faces must have looked pretty confused. She smiles again, chuckling her gravelly chuckle. Then she looks at us very seriously as if she is weighing whether or not she can trust us.

"The boy is possessed," she says. Joel and I sit down, and now we're the ones who are shaking. Nobody has said anything about Tyler being possessed except us on the way to the rink. It's as if she's read our minds.

We watch the game in silence for a bit, glancing back and forth at each other. A fight breaks out at the other end of the rink, catching everyone's attention. Tyler, his temper getting the better of him, gets a penalty for being the third man in. When we turn to see what the woman will say about this, she's gone.

"It's not such a big deal," says Joel. "I mean, somebody always says geniuses are possessed sooner or later. We said it sooner and she said it later."

But he knows and I know that that isn't what's bothering us. There was something about the look on her face and the way she said it that wasn't the same as the way we had, joking about it on the way to the game. She meant it.

"Hit me with your best shot," says Joel. He's suited up on the minirink in his backyard. I put everything

I've got into a drive. *Thwack*. The puck lifts and lifts, sailing over Joel's head and over the fence into his neighbor's yard. A dog back there barks. Joel glares.

"You're possessed," he says, banging his stick against the goalposts.

"It's the puck," I say.

"Right," says Joel. "The puck is now possessed by Sparky. He's got more pucks than we do."

"Hey," I tell him. "You've got a zero goals-against. What're you complaining about?"

"You only got three shots on the net," he says, pulling off his helmet.

It's cold so we head inside. Joel's dad is filling a lunch pail with about twelve roast-beef sandwiches. He works the night shift at a factory.

"Gonna catch the big game tonight?" he asks. We both nod. Sacred Heart is coming into town. And Tyler Taylor is now on a seven-game shutout streak. It's a rare night game for a high school team, rescheduled so more folks can come out.

"There's talk that *Sports Illustrated* has sent up a reporter," says Joel's dad, cutting up some pickles. "Wish I could be there."

"There'll probably be NHL scouts," says Joel as he zaps us a couple of Cup-A-Soups.

"What do you know about Tyler's father?" I ask.

Joel's dad shakes his head. "A real hard case," he says. "I went to school with Randy."

"What happened to him?"

I watch Joel's dad take a pie out of the fridge and cut himself a large hunk. Cherry. He licks the flat of the knife and chucks it in the sink. There's a bit of cherry on the corner of his lip. It looks like blood.

"Well, most people figure he was wiped out by the mob for his gambling debts. Oh, it was big-time stuff for a small town like this. There's no proof, mind you. They never found his body. Some people figure he just ran out on Carrie and the boy and didn't leave a forwarding address. There were rumors of him having another woman."

Joel and I look at each other, remembering the crackpot lady at the game.

"What do you think happened?" I ask.

Joel's dad thinks for a minute. "I think the mob got him," he says. "You wanna know why?" He checks the clock and then leans back on the counter, cleaning off his hands. We're sitting at the breakfast table with our Cup-A-Soups at our lips, just waiting.

"Because—mean scumbucket that Randy could be—I can't see how he would have missed the big ceremony even if he'd had to crawl to it."

"The big ceremony?"

"The unveiling of The Ghost."

Joel and I remember the photographs up in the snack area of the arena. But we've never looked very closely at them.

"You mean," says Joel, "that's when he disappeared?"

His dad nods. "I'll never forget it. Boy, the talent that was here in town. The Rocket, Howe, Stasiak, Bathgate, Armstrong, Lindberger. Some of the old-timers and some of the new stars—the Great One himself."

Joel and I can hardly believe our ears. Gretzky!

Joel's dad laughs. "It was the off-season. A lot of guys wanted to pay tribute to The Ghost. Eddy Longo was a guy who really loved hockey—had a good time. It was a game to him. I remember Howe sayin' that at the ceremony.

"Eddy looked great that day. A real gentleman, in his eighties by then but pretty chipper. You should have seen it. Actually, you did, Joelly, now that I remember. You were there."

Joel just about chokes on that one. "I was?"

His dad looks pleased. "Yep," he says. "In a pack on my back."

"I saw the Great One here in town?" Joel has put his cup down. You can see by the look in his eye that he's trying hard to remember it.

"I oughta know," says his dad. "I was the one lugging you around. You were just over one year old."

Joel's dad takes a king-sized thermos and fills it with coffee from the percolator. "I remember seeing young Tyler there. He'd have been about four or five. He was holding Carrie's hand—cute little tyke—and every now and then his granddad Carl would pick him up and show him off. When The Ghost pulled the rope that unveiled the statue, I think Carl handed the boy to him. Yeah, it was in the papers. This spry old hockey legend beaming out at the crowd, holding his great-grandson. Made a lovely picture. The only thing that ruined the picture was Randy not being there. I guess the family tried not to notice."

There is silence for a minute or so. I take a slurp

of soup. "I heard some guys at the rink say the mob guys dragged Randy away from the dinner table, right in front of Mrs. Longo and Tyler."

"There's all kinds of tales about what happened," says Joel's dad, packing up his midnight lunch. "He wasn't in town much in those days. He was playing for one of the new expansion teams—Philly, maybe. He and Carrie weren't really together anymore, but he had come up for the ceremony. I saw him myself in town a day or two before the unveiling. Seemed pretty strung out. And then—poof—he was gone. That's why I think they got him."

Joel and I stand looking up at the big bronze of Eddy Longo. It's about half an hour to game time. The arena lights give The Ghost a long shadow that stretches down the path toward the parking lot. He's bigger than ever in this light.

Then we see Tyler coming across the lot, his feet sticking out, his arms swinging, his jacket wide open. He's got his own shadow swaggering along behind him, head down. He passes through his great-grandfather's shadow and comes out into the light, where he reaches out to rub the cold shiny toe.

Suddenly he notices us and his eyes get shifty, as if we might just have a puck or two on us somewhere, maybe hidden in a pocket ready to hurl in his direction, and he's got to be ready to snag it. Anytime, anywhere. It suddenly feels a lot colder, and Joel and I head inside.

And she is there again. In the same flea-bitten furs. She doesn't look like she's changed her makeup since last week. She's sitting alone. We wave as we take our seats, sort of as a joke. She turns away.

The place is packed. Sacred Heart is in second place in the county. They lost to Christ the King 1–0 in the first game of the season. They haven't lost since.

The game starts fast and tough. Before five minutes are up, the Hearts have had four solid shots on Tyler.

"He looks scared to death," says Joel to me nervously, as we watch the goalie regroup after a close call.

"TY-*LER*, TY-*LER*, TY-*LER*." The whole arena is chanting. Maybe it's because of all that foot stamping that we didn't notice the weird woman moving. Suddenly she's poking her face between Joel and me again.

"As scared as if he's seen a ghost," she says.

Joel and I just about jump out of our skins.

"Who are you?" I ask, before I can stop myself.

She looks at us closely. We can hear the game start up behind us again, but she seems to hold us hypnotized. She's sizing us up.

"His old man's got a hold on him," she says. "He did the same to me, but I got over it. Something's gotta be done."

By now Joel has recovered a bit from the surprise attack. He says, "Well, I hope no one ever tries to unpossess me from being the greatest goalie in the world."

She stares at Joel as if she can't comprehend what he's talking about.

"What do you mean, exactly?" I ask her. Behind us the game goes on, back and forth. Back and forth. But something has been on my mind since the first time we met the woman, and suddenly I know what it is. "Tyler's real father—is he back?"

The woman looks at me keenly, then at Joel. "He never left," she says. I feel a chill climb up my spine. She doesn't seem drunk tonight. "Randy's been around this arena ever since he vanished." She throws her hands up into the air like a magician, as if she's just scattered Randy Longo all over us in tiny invisible pieces of confetti. I pull back, startled, and actually look around in the air for something. Then I feel stupid.

"This is crazy," says Joel. He turns back to the game, but I can't.

"In the arena?" I ask her.

"Watching," she says. "Watching."

I nod, as if I understand. What I think I understand is that this woman is really and truly nuts, and it might be a good idea to play along with her until the intermission and then find somewhere else to sit. Still nodding, I turn slowly toward the ice, catching Joel's eye as I do. He raises his eyebrows.

I try to tune in the game, but it seems far away somehow. I can feel the woman behind us. I can hear her raspy breathing if I listen close enough. Then she starts to talk—mumble, more like. She's going on about Randy Longo. About Randy and her. About the fun of it, at first, when he was still playing. Then about his temper. I watch Sacred Heart passing the puck, shooting on net. I watch Tyler block his twelfth shot, his thirteenth. And all the time the woman behind us carries on without raising her voice.

"Then he started gambling," she says. "That's what got him. Not just in the ordinary way. Sure he lost money now and then—that wasn't so bad. But he was not a man who could stand losing. That was his big problem. He refused to see it. He got himself in deep with all the wrong kinds of people. People who only know one way to solve a problem."

The puck is out to center ice, but Sacred Heart is on a roll. They steal the puck back from Christ the King.

"In order to be truly great," says the woman, "you have to be able to lose now and then. The great ones learn early. They play to win, but they can handle losing. Put it behind them. Separate the bad moments out. They can smile about it. Not right away, but the next day. You see?"

Even as she is saying it, the Sacred Hearts are all around the net, with less than a minute in the period, swinging and chopping at the loose puck. The crowd is on its feet. I rise with them in time to see Tyler scoop the puck off the ice and, at the same time, take a mighty swipe with his goalie stick at the nearest Heart, hitting him hard across the back of his legs. I watch the player crumple like a water buffalo with a lion on its back. The whistle blows.

"This is the greatest goalie in the world?" The woman says it quietly, but loud enough for Joel and

antom of the opera," says
uilding in some secret hide-
Tyler plays." My eyes scan

ed," says Joel. But he looks

r they close—"
Anyway, she didn't say he
around it, whatever that
as I am.
e. A janitor locks the door
for a moment, watching
head up the path toward
hard to tell with the snow
ts pointing up—throwing
e woman said, The Ghost

me," says Joel.
d, but I find myself shiv-

ther's skates, so the mob

und the top of the pants,
where the two parts of
her.
let out a string of swear

looks scared.
say. "The statue—"
s my arm.

me to hear over the hollering of the hometown crowd as Tyler Taylor is ejected from the game.

That's when Joel loses it. "See what you did!" he shouts at her. "You unpossessed him, all right—you *hexed* him. What are you, a witch or something?"

"No," she says.

"Well, you look like one," says Joel.

I know Joel pretty well. I bet the second he said it, he wished he hadn't. I sure did. But I can't think of anything to say. The woman looks down at her hands. Her nails are gross—too long and too red and all exactly the same shape. Suddenly she just looks pathetic.

"I'm sorry," says Joel. "It's just that . . . it's just that . . ." But he can't think what it just is. The buzzer buzzes noisily to end the period. There is no score in the game, but with the unsportsmanlike penalty to Tyler, with him out of the game, it might as well be 6–0 for Sacred Heart.

"I'll get out of your hair, boys," says the woman. Neither of us say anything to stop her. "But I'd like you to do something for me."

"What?" I ask. Somehow I feel we owe her.

"You tell your friend Tyler Taylor next time you see him that if he's going to go getting himself possessed, he better dump the spirit of that rascal father of his and let the spirit of The Ghost get inside him and do the job *right*."

It takes a minute for Joel and me to figure it out.

"He rubs The Ghost's toe every time he comes to play," says Joel.

The woman nods. "I seen him," she says. "I seen him. But that's idol worship. Don't people know the difference anymore? Don't you boys know your Bible? Idol worship is all wrong. You gotta look up. If that boy looked up at that statue of Eddy out there, he'd see the old man smiling. He's having himself one whale of a time, Eddy Longo. But Tyler's too much like his own father. Randy never looked up, either. That's how he got blind-sided."

She smiles a little as she gathers herself up to leave, but it's a sad smile. "He couldn't fill his grandfather's skates," she says. "So the mob went and did it for him." Now she laughs out loud—big and loud—and that brings on a fit of coughing. She doubles over and we back off, afraid she's going to spew. When she recovers, she doesn't even look back at us, just wobbles out of the bleachers on her salt-stained heels.

I want to say that we don't even know Tyler and there's no way we're going to pass on some message from a crazy lady, *especially* if she used to be his dad's girlfriend. She's leaving, and that's really what I want now. For her to go. It's stupid, but it's like Joel and I want to blame her for what happened to Tyler, as if she really did hex him in some way. Something did.

Then I remember the look on his face before the game. He'd been spooked all along.

We watch the rest of the game in a kind of glum silence. The backup goalie for Christ the King is good but not good enough. Sacred Heart wins the game 1–0. Tyler still has himself a zero goals-against average, but it's just not the same anymore.

"What is it?" says Joel

"Maybe he's like the
me. "Maybe he's in the b
out watching every gam
the rafters.

"Now she's got you spo
around, too.

"Maybe if we stayed a
"Forget it!" says Joel.
was *in* the arena. Jus
means." Joel's as spooke

We're the last ones to l
behind us. We stand th
the snow swirl around.
the statue of The Ghost.
in our eyes and the spotl
weird shadows—but, lik
seems to be smiling.

"Looks kind of devilish

I'm not sure if it's the
ering.

*He couldn't fill his gra
did it for him.*

I lower my eyes. There
like a corded belt, is a b
the statue were welded t

Before I can even thin
words.

"What is it?" asks Joel

"Those pictures in the
"What?" says Joel. He

"The statue's hollow," I say.

"Yeah," he says. "So—"

Then he begins to know, too. He looks at the line where the statue was joined together. "Randy was in town that week. That's what Dad said." Then Joel is grabbing onto me. Tightly. *"He's in there?"*

It all makes a gruesome kind of sense—everything the weird lady was saying. And yet, who put the statue together? Joel must be thinking the same thing as me.

"The mob," he says.

For another minute we try to imagine it. Then Joel punches me in the arm. "Let's get out of here," he says.

But even as we turn to leave, we hear a door open somewhere in the dark behind us, and out from the side of the building a shadowy figure appears. Even before we can see him clearly, we both know who it is. We've been watching this guy all winter.

"Are you gonna say something?" whispers Joel.

"About this?" I whisper, pointing at the statue. But Joel is watching Tyler walk away, and he makes up his mind for us.

"Tough call," he cries. He wants it to sound friendly, like we're on his side. Mostly it just sounds nervous.

Tyler turns around and looks our way. He doesn't say a thing, just stares. He doesn't move.

"Your zero goals-against is still intact," says Joel. I can't believe he's doing this.

"What do you want?" Tyler says.

We don't move. I look at Joel. He can't think of anything more to say.

Then Tyler comes toward us. He squints through the snowflakes on his lashes. "You guys again," he says.

"We were looking at the statue of The Ghost," I say. It sounds pretty dumb. I wonder if Tyler can hear the shaking in my voice. He doesn't look at the statue.

"Coach says I had it coming," says Tyler. He doesn't sound angry, just kind of dull on the edges, like last year's skates. We kind of shrug.

"Coach says I'm lucky they didn't throw me out for the season." We shrug again. I have the feeling Tyler really wants to talk, but I can't think of what to say. I feel dizzy.

Tyler looks puzzled, then he turns to go.

"Do something," says Joel.

"No!"

"You've got to!" he whispers frantically.

"Tell a guy I know where his dad's dead body is?"

Tyler couldn't have heard what I said, but he stops and turns around. "What's going on?" he says.

"This is a great statue," I say, before I know what I'm doing.

Tyler is coming back and Joel is grabbing my arm so hard that I can feel his fingernails right through my jacket. Right through his gloves.

"Have you ever noticed how he smiles?" I say. "The Ghost, I mean."

I can almost feel Joel wince. I look up. I look back at Tyler. But he's still not interested in looking up. He looks like he's more interested in punching out my lights.

"Who are you guys?" he says. "You making fun of me?"

His face looks angry, but there's something else there. He's tired; that's part of it. And sad or something. Like he's got an ache in his gut. I take a quick glance back up at the statue.

"They say Eddy Longo loved the game." I almost choke on that. I look at Joel. He looks at me, at Tyler, at the statue, panic-stricken. Then nobody speaks. There's hardly any sound. Just the four of us standing there—Tyler, Joel, me and The Ghost—in the thickly falling snow.

And in the silence I think I hear a sound. Not the traffic up on Delaney. Nearby. I look at Joel. He looks at me. There it is again, and it's coming from the statue. Like a finger on a window.

Tap, tap.

Joel crowds close to me, almost knocking me over.

Tap, tap.

We both look at Tyler to see if he's heard it, but it seems like he's in a trance. He's looking up, trying to make out the smile on his great-grandfather's cold bronze face.

"I don't," he murmurs. I'm not even sure he's talking to us.

"Don't what?" I ask.

"Don't love hockey."

Tap. Tap. Tap.

There is no mistaking it this time. Joel groans. Tyler doesn't seem to notice. He seems far away. He's looking up into the snow.

"So give yourself a break," I tell him. "Lighten up."

"Yeah," says Joel. "Lighten up."

Suddenly, it's as if Tyler has remembered where he is and who he's talking to—a couple of nobodies. "You're telling *me* to lighten up?" he says.

Tap, tap. Tap, tap.

He must have heard it that time. But he's smiling. Smiling at us.

"You're the guys who should lighten up," he says. "You look like you've seen a ghost."

"Not seen," mumbles Joel, but the words are lost in my shoulder where his face is buried.

Tyler chuckles, and before I know what's happening, he reaches out and grabs me by the arm.

And I scream.

I don't mean to scream. It's the suddenness of it. I scream and then Joel screams and we both jump away from him as if he's got a blowtorch in his hands.

He steps back. He holds up his hands. "Hey," he says. "What is it with you two?"

That's when Joel loses it for the second time that night.

"It's you," he says. "You scared us. You're a scary guy, Tyler."

Tyler does nothing for a moment. Then he nods. He looks down.

"He didn't really mean that," I say. "We're just a little freaked out. Must have been the game."

"Yeah," says Joel. "The game."

Tyler looks at us again. At Joel. His face looks a bit calmer. "You know, this is weird," he says. "But you're the second person's said that to me tonight. About being scary, I mean."

Joel and I are thinking the same thing. But we're wrong.

"The coach said it to me," he says. "Maybe he's right."

He looks up at Eddy Longo. I can feel my heart going crazy. Joel and I are holding our breath.

"Eddy," says Tyler. "Is this thing all getting too scary?"

Tap, tap, tap, tap.

We all hear it this time. Tyler looks at us, startled. We stare back at him. "Can you beat that," he says. "He talked to me."

Then he laughs out loud.

Joel and I exchange glances.

"The Ghost talked to me." He laughs. "I guess I should listen, eh?"

Joel and I nod. Then Tyler laughs again. He reaches out and rubs the shiny toe. We all laugh a bit. Then the laughter peters away.

"Will you guys be at the next game?" he says. We nod.

"St. John's," says Joel. He knows the schedule by heart.

Tyler nods. He looks down and kicks at the snow a bit. "If only I knew how to let the pressure off," he says. "Should we ask The Ghost what he thinks?"

"No!" says Joel.

"I think one message is enough," I add quickly. "I mean, for one night."

Tyler suddenly shivers and pulls his jacket together. He buttons it up, brushes the snow off his Christ the King crest. "Maybe it's time to let one get by me," he says. He looks at us suspiciously, as if we might think what he has said is weird. But it doesn't sound weird to us. Not tonight.

"One for The Ghost," says Joel.

"Right." He's glad we understand. "Don't tell anyone I said that."

"No way," says Joel. I second the motion.

Then Tyler Taylor smiles at us. It's not a great smile. He could use some lessons. He turns and walks across the parking lot, his feet sticking out, his arms swinging, swaggering like a pirate until he disappears into the snowy dark. We pause only for a second, but it turns out to be one second too long.

Tap, tap, tap.

And we're out of there! Arms swinging like mad.

Later, when we talk about it, we both agree that the laugh that followed us *must* have been our imagination.

☜ Dawn

Barnsey met Dawn on the night bus to North Bay. His mother put him on at Ottawa, just after supper. His parents owned a store and the Christmas season was frantic, so for the third year in a row, Barnsey was going up to Grandma Barrymore's and his parents would follow Christmas day. He had cousins in North Bay, so it was fine with Barnsey, as long as he didn't have to sit beside someone weird the whole way.

"What if I have to sit beside someone weird the whole way?" he asked his mother in the bus terminal. She cast him a warning look. A let's-not-make-a-scene look. Barnsey figured she was in a hurry to get back to the store.

"You are thirteen, Matthew," she said. There was an edge in her voice that hadn't been there before. "Has anything bad happened to you yet?"

Barnsey was picking out a couple of magazines for the trip: *Guitar World* and *Sports Illustrated*. "I didn't say anything *bad* was going to happen. If anything *bad* happens, I make a racket and the bus driver deals with it. I know all that. I'm just talking about someone weird."

"For instance?" said his mother.

"Someone who smells. Someone really, really fat who spills over onto my seat. Someone who wants to talk about her liver operation."

His mother paid for the magazines and threw in a Kit Kat, too. Barnsey didn't remind her that she'd already bought him a Kit Kat, and let him buy a Coke, chips and some gum. And this was apart from the healthy stuff she had already packed at home. She was usually pretty strict about junk food.

"I just asked," said Barnsey.

"Come on," said his mother, giving his shoulder a bit of a squeeze. "Or the only *weird* person you're going to be sitting beside is your mother on the way back to the store."

Barnsey didn't bother to ask if that was an option. His parents put a lot of stock in planning. They didn't put much stock in spontaneity.

"What if I end up in Thunder Bay by mistake?"

His mother put her arm around him. He was almost as tall as she was now. "Matthew," she said in her let's-be-rational voice. "That would require quite a mistake on your part. But, if it were to happen, you have a good head on your shoulders *and* your own bank card."

His mother almost looked as if she was going to say something about how they had always encouraged him to be independent, but luckily she noticed it was boarding time.

They were at Bay 6, and his mother suddenly gave him a very uncharacteristic hug. A bear hug. They weren't a hugging kind of a family. She looked him in the eyes.

"Matthew," she said. "It's not so long. Remember that."

"I know," said Barnsey. But he wasn't sure if his mother meant the trip or the time before he'd see her again. He couldn't tell.

They moved through the line toward the driver, who was taking tickets at the door of the bus.

"Don't do the thing with the money," Barnsey whispered to his mother.

"Why not?" she said. Barnsey didn't answer. "It's just good business. And besides, young man, I'll do what I please."

And she did. As Barnsey gave the driver his ticket, Barnsey's mother ripped a twenty-dollar bill in half ceremoniously in front of the driver's face. She gave half the bill to Barnsey, who shoved it quickly in his pocket.

"Here, my good man," said his mother to the bus driver in her store voice. "My son will give you the other half upon arrival in North Bay. Merry Christmas."

The driver thanked her. But he gave Barnsey a secret kind of cockeyed look, as if to say, Does she pull this kind of stunt all the time?

Then Barnsey was on board the bus, and there was Dawn.

There was no other seat. His mother had once told him that if there weren't any seats left, the bus company would have to get a bus just for him. That was the way they did business. So Barnsey shuffled up and down the bus a couple of times even after he'd put his bag up top, looking—hoping—that someone would take the seat beside Dawn so he could triumphantly demand a bus of his own. But there were no other seats and no other passengers.

He suddenly wanted very much to go back out to his mother, even though she would say he was being irrational. But then when he caught a glimpse of her through the window, she looked almost as miserable as he felt. He remembered the bear hug with a shiver. It shook his resolve. Timidly he turned to Dawn.

"Is this seat taken?" he asked.

The girl took off her Walkman earphones and stared at the seat a bit, as if looking for someone. She took a long time.

"Doesn't look like it."

Barnsey sat down and made himself comfortable. He got out his own Walkman and arranged his tapes on his lap and thought about the order in which he was going to eat all the junk he had or whether he'd eat a bit of each thing—the chocolate bars, the chips, the Coke—in some kind of order so they all came out even. At home his mother had packed a loganberry soda and some trail mix. He'd keep those for last. Strictly emergency stuff.

Then the bus driver came on board and they were off.

"There's talk of big snow up the valley a way, so I'm gonna light a nice cozy fire," he said. People chuckled. There was already a cozy kind of nighttime we're-stuck-in-this-together mood on the bus. Nobody was drunk or too loud. And the girl beside Barnsey seemed to be completely engrossed in whatever was coming through her earphones.

It was only the way she looked that he had any problem with. The nine earrings, the nose rings and the Mohawk in particular—orange along the scalp and purple along the crest as if her skull was a planet and the sun was coming up on the horizon of her head. She was about twenty and dressed all in black, with clunky black Doc Martens. But as long as she was just going to listen to her music, then Barnsey would listen to his and everything would be fine.

And it was for the first hour or so. By then the bus had truly slipped into a comfortable humming silence. It was about nine, and some people were sleeping. Others were talking softly as if they didn't want to wake a baby in the next room. That's when the mix-up occurred.

There isn't much room in a bus seat. And there wasn't much room on Barnsey's lap. Somehow a couple of his tapes slid off him into the space between him and Dawn, the girl with the horizon on her head, though he didn't know her name yet. The weird thing was, the same thing had happened to her tapes. And the weirdest thing of all was that they both found out at just about the same time.

Barnsey shoved the new Xiphoid Process tape into his machine and punched it on. While he was waiting for the music to start, he dug the cassette out from his backpack and looked again at the hologram cover. The band was standing under lowering skies all around an eerie-looking gravestone. Then if you tipped the cover just right, the guys all seemed to pull back, and there was a hideous ghoul all covered with dirt and worms standing right in the middle of them where the grave marker had been. It was great.

Barnsey pulled a bag of chips from the backpack at his feet, squeezed it so that the pressure in the bag made it pop open and crunched on a couple of chips as quietly as he could. He was busy enjoying the way the first sour cream and onion chip tastes, and it took him a minute to notice he wasn't hearing anything.

He turned the volume up a bit. Nothing. Then he realized there *was* something. A tinkling noise and a bit of a whooshing noise, and a bit of what sounded like rain and some dripping and more tinkling.

Barnsey banged his Walkman. He thought the batteries were dying. Then Dawn changed tapes as well and suddenly yelled, as if she'd just touched a hot frying pan. Some people looked around angrily. The looks on their faces made Barnsey think they had just been waiting for a chance to glare at her. One lady glanced at him, too, in a pitying kind of way, as if to say, Poor young thing. Having to sit beside a banshee like that.

Meanwhile, both of them opened up their Walkmans like Christmas presents. They held their tapes up to the little lights above them to check the titles.

"Rain Forest with Temple Bells?" Barnsey read out loud.

" 'Scream for Your Supper!' " Dawn read out loud.

Barnsey apologized, nervously. Dawn just laughed. They made the switch, but before Barnsey could even say thank you, the girl suddenly took his tape back.

"Tell you what," she said. "You listen to that fer 'alf a mo, and I'll give this a try. 'Kay?"

She had a thick accent, British.

"Okay," said Barnsey, "but I think yours is broken or something."

She took her tape back and tried it. She smiled, and her smile was good. It kind of stretched across her face and curled up at the ends.

"Naa," she said. "Ya just 'av ta listen, mate. Closely, like."

So Barnsey listened closely. He turned it up. There was a rain forest. There were ravens croaking and other birds twittering away. And there were bells. He thought someone was playing them, but after a while he realized that it was just the rain playing them, the wind. He kept waiting for the music to start. He didn't know what the music would be. Any moment a drum would kick in, he thought, then a synthesizer all warbly and a guitar keening high and distorted and a thumping bass and, last of all, a voice. Maybe singing about trees. About saving them.

But no drum kicked in. Maybe the tape *was* broken?

It took him a minute to realize Dawn was tapping him on the shoulder. She had his Xiphoid Process tape in her hand and a cranky look on her face.

"This is killer-diller," she said.

"You like X.P.?" he asked.

"It's rubbish."

Barnsey laughed. *Rubbish*. What a great word. He pulled out Rain Forest with Temple Bells.

"What ya think?" she asked.

"It's rubbish."

Then they both started to giggle. And now people stared at them as if they were in cahoots and going to ruin the whole trip for everyone. Dawn hit him on the arm to shush him up.

He showed her the hologram cover of the X.P. tape.

"You think it's their mum?" she asked.

"Maybe," he said. He wished he could think of something to say. He just flipped the picture a few times. She leaned toward him. Her hand out.

"Dawn," she whispered.

It took him a minute to realize she was introducing herself. "Barnsey," he whispered back, as if it was a code. He shook her hand.

He offered her some chips. She took the whole bag and made a big deal of holding it up to the light so she could read the ingredients. She shuddered.

"It's a bleedin' chemical plant in 'ere," she said.

"Rubbish," said Barnsey. Then he dug out the trail mix and offered it to Dawn, and they both settled down to listen to their own tapes. Barnsey turned X.P. down to 2 because there was no way Dawn would be able to hear her forest with Spice-box wailing on the guitar and Mickey Slick pounding on the drums. After a couple of cuts he switched it off altogether.

He found himself thinking of the time he had traveled with his father out to British Columbia, where he was from, to Denman Island. He remembered the forest there, like nothing he'd ever seen in southern Ontario. Vast and high. It had been a lovely summer day with the light sifting down through the trees. But, he thought, if it rained there, it would sound like Dawn's tape.

He didn't put a tape in his cassette. He left the earphones on and listened to the hum of the bus instead.

"It's not so long."

It was the bus driver. Barnsey woke up with his mouth feeling like the inside of a bread box.

There was a stirring all around. People waking, stretching, chattering sleepily and my-my-ing as they looked out the windows. The bus was stopped.

"Will ya lookit that," said Dawn. Her nose was pressed up against the window. Outside was a nothingness of white.

They had pulled off the highway into a football field–sized parking lot. Another bus was parked up ahead. Through the swirling blizzard they could see lots of trucks and cars in the lot. It wasn't the stop Barnsey remembered from previous trips.

Barnsey could see the driver standing outside without his jacket, his shoulders hunched against the driving snow. He was talking to another bus driver, nodding his head a lot and stamping his feet to keep warm. Then he hopped back on the bus and closed the door behind him.

"Seems like we've got ourselves a little unscheduled

stop," he said. "The road's bunged up clear through to Mattawa."

Someone asked him a question. Somebody interrupted with another question. The driver did a lot of answering and nodding and shaking his head and reassuring. Barnsey just looked over Dawn's shoulder at the outside, shivering a bit from sleepiness and the sight of all that whirling snow. Dawn smelled nice. Not exotic like the perfume his mother wore, but kind of bracing and clean.

"This here place doesn't have a name," said the driver. People laughed. He was making it all sound like fun. "But the barn there with all the blinking lights is called the Cattle Yard, and the owner says y'all er welcome to come on down and warm yerself up a spell."

Passengers immediately started to get up and stretch and fish around for handbags and sweaters and things. There was an air of excitement on the bus. The Cattle Yard was a big roadhouse painted fire-engine red and lit up with spotlights. It was no ordinary way station.

Still sleepy, Barnsey made no effort to move as people started to file past him, pulling on their coats. Dawn still had her nose pressed up against the glass.

"D'ya know where I spent last Christmas?" she said. Barnsey thought for a moment, as if maybe she'd told him and he'd forgotten.

"In Bethlehem," she said.

"*The* Bethlehem?"

"That's right," she said. "In a bar."

Barnsey looked at Dawn. She was smiling but not like she was fooling. "There are bars in Bethlehem?"

She laughed. "Brilliant bars. Smashing litt'l town is Bethlehem."

Barnsey tried to imagine it.

Then the bus driver was beside him. "Here, you might need this," he said. And with a flick of his fingers he produced the half-a-twenty Barnsey's mother had given him. Barnsey was about to explain that it was meant to be a tip, but the driver waved his hand in protest. "Just don't get yourself all liquored up, son," he said, and then, laughing and clapping Barnsey on the back, he headed out of the bus.

"Wha's that then?" asked Dawn, looking at the half-a-twenty-dollar bill. Barnsey pulled the other half out of his pants pocket and held them side by side.

"Hungry?" he said.

And she was hungry. He hadn't realized how skinny she was, but she stored away a grilled cheese sandwich in no time and two pieces of apple pie with ice cream. She ordered hot water and fished a tea bag from deep in her ratty black leather jacket.

"Ginseng, mate," she said. "Nothing illegal."

But Barnsey had only been noticing how stained the tea bag was and the little tab at the end of the string which had strange characters written on it.

It was all so strange. Strange for Barnsey to walk into a place with her, as if they were on a date—a thirteen-year-old and a twenty-year-old. He wondered if people thought she was his sister. He couldn't imagine his parents putting up with the way Dawn looked. She sure turned heads at the Cattle Yard. He wasn't sure if he minded or not. In his burgundy L. L. Bean coat, he didn't exactly look like he belonged in the place, either.

It was a huge smoke-filled bar with moose antlers on the knotty pine walls and two or three big TVs around the room tuned into the Nashville Network. There was a Leafs game on the TV over the bar. Just about everyone was wearing a trucker's hat, and nobody looked like they were leaving until maybe Christmas.

The bus passengers were herded down to one end where a section had been closed off but was now reopened. The bus drivers smoked and made phone calls and made jokes to their passengers about not getting on the wrong bus when they left and ending up in Timbuktu. Through the window and the blizzard of snow, Barnsey watched another bus roll in.

"I saw three ships cum sailin' in," sang Dawn. She was picking at Barnsey's leftover french fries—*chips*, she called them—trying to find ones that didn't have any burger juice on them. She was a vegetarian.

"Bloody heathen," she'd called him when he'd ordered a bacon burger and fries. He loved that.

"I've gotta go find the loo," she said.

"Bloody heathen," he said.

She flicked him on the nose with a chip as she clomped by in her Doc Martens. He wondered if it was possible to walk quietly in them.

"Rubbish," he said. He watched her walk through the bar toward the rest rooms. Somebody must have said something to her because she suddenly stopped and turned back to a table where five guys in trucking caps were sitting. They looked like all together they probably weighed a ton, but that didn't seem to bother Dawn. She leaned up close to one of them, her fists curled menacingly, and snarled something right at his face.

Barnsey watched in horror, imagining a scene from some movie where the whole place would erupt into a beer-slinging, window-smashing brawl. Instead, the guy whose face she was talking at suddenly roared with laughter and slapped the tabletop. The other four guys laughed, too. One of them ended up spitting half a mug of beer all over his friends. Then Dawn shook hands with her tormentors and sauntered off to the loo, as she called it.

Barnsey felt like he would burst with admiration. He picked up her teacup and smelled the ginseng. It smelled deadly. The writing on the little tab was Indian, he guessed. From India.

He looked around. On the big TV a country songstress with big country hair and dressed in a beautiful country-blue dress was draping silver tinsel on a Christmas tree while she sang about somebody being home for Christmas. Then the image would cut to that somebody in a pickup fighting his way through a blizzard. Same boat we're in, thought Barnsey. Then the image would cut back to the Christmas tree and then to a flashback of the couple walking up a country road with a bouncy dog, having an argument in the rain and so on. Then back to the guy in the truck, the girl by the tree. It was a whole little minimovie.

Barnsey found himself trying to imagine X.P. dressing that same tinsely Christmas tree in that nice living room. But of course the guy in the truck trying to get home for Christmas would be the grim reaper or something, with worms crawling out of its eyes.

Then Dawn came back.

"What did you say to that guy?" Barnsey asked.

She smiled mysteriously. "I told 'im that if 'e'd said what 'e said to me in Afghanistan, 'e'd 'ave to marry me on the spot."

It was around eleven before word came through that it was safe to leave. The drivers got everybody sorted out and back on board. Everyone at the Cattle Yard yelled Merry Christmas and held up their beer glasses in a toast. The guy who had been rude to Dawn stood and bowed as she passed by, and she curtsied. Then she made as if she was going to bite off his nose, which made his ton of friends roar again, their fat guts shaking with laughter.

By then Barnsey knew that Dawn had just got back from Nepal, where she'd been traveling with " 'er mate" ever since she left Israel, where she'd been working on a kibbutz after arriving there from Bloody Cairo, where she'd had all her kit stolen. Before that she'd been in Ghana and before that art school. Barnsey didn't know what a kit was, or a kibbutz. He wasn't sure where Nepal was, either, or what or who 'er mate might be. But he didn't ask. She'd called him mate, too.

On the bus the excitement of the unscheduled stop

soon died down. The roads were only passable so it was slow going. It was kind of nice that the three buses were traveling together. In a convoy, the driver had called it. It sounded reassuring. Soon people were falling asleep, snoring. But not Barnsey. He sat thinking. Trying to imagine working on a flower farm in Israel, the heat, the fragrance of it. Trying to imagine Bethlehem.

"Was it cold?"

"Freezin' at night," she said.

"See any stables?"

She laughed. "No, but I did see a good-sized shed behind a McDonald's."

Barnsey laughed. He tried to imagine the holy family pulling into Bethlehem today and huddling down in a shed out back of a McDonald's. Maybe Joseph would have a Big Mac. But Mary? Probably a vegetarian, he decided.

Quietness again.

"What kind of a store is it your people 'ave, master Barnsey?"

"A gift store," he said.

"Ah, well," said Dawn. "I can imagine a gift store would be busy at Christmas."

Finally, Barnsey dozed off. And the next thing he knew, the bus was slowing down and driving through the deserted streets of North Bay. It was past 2:00 A.M.

"That'll be 'er," said Dawn as they pulled into the bus terminal. Somehow she had recognized his grandma Barrymore in the little knot of worried folks waiting.

Barnsey just sat drowsily for a minute while people stirred around him. He felt like he weighed a ton.

"Get on with ya," said Dawn in a cheery voice. And she made a big joke of shoving him and roughhousing him out of his seat as if he was Dumbo the elephant. Then she gathered up all his wrappers and cans and threw them at him, saying, " 'Ere—lookit this! Yer not leavin' this for me, I 'ope." Barnsey found himself, weak with laughter, herded down the aisle. At the door he said good-bye and hoped that her trip to Vancouver would be nothing but rubbish the whole way. Grandma Barrymore was standing at the foot of the bus stairs. Much to her surprise, Dawn grabbed Barnsey by the head and scrubbed it hard with her knuckle.

"In Afghanistan, you'd have to marry me for that," said Barnsey.

"Toodle-oo, mate," said Dawn, blowing him a kiss. She blew one at Grandma Barrymore, too.

Dawn would arrive in Vancouver on Christmas Eve. Barnsey thought of her often over the next couple of days. He'd check his watch and imagine her arriving in Winnipeg, although all he knew of Winnipeg was the Blue Bombers football stadium that he'd seen on TV. And then Regina and Calgary. He imagined the three buses like wise men still traveling across the country in a convoy. But as much as Barnsey thought about Dawn, he gave up trying to talk to anyone about her. Grandma had seen her but only long enough to get the wrong impression. And when Barnsey tried to tell his cousins about her, it came out like a cartoon, with her wacky hair and her fat black boots. He couldn't get Dawn across to them—the *life* of her—only the image of her, so he stopped trying.

There was a lot to do, anyway. His cousins had arranged a skating party and Grandma wanted him to go shopping with her and help with some chores around the house. He enjoyed all the attention she showered on him. She spoiled him rotten just the way she'd spoiled his father rotten, she liked to say. But he'd never noticed it quite so much as this year. Anything he looked at, she asked him if he wanted it. It was spooky.

Then it was Christmas morning. It was a four-hour drive from Ottawa. His parents would arrive by 1:00 P.M. and that's when the celebration would start. When he saw his father's Mustang coming up the driveway at 10:30 A.M., Barnsey knew something was wrong.

He didn't go to the door. He watched from the window. They should have come in the big car. But there wasn't any they. Just his dad.

"Matthew, go help your dad with his parcels," said Grandma.

"No," said Barnsey. He was remembering the last time he had looked at his mother in the bus terminal, through the window. The look on her face. "It won't be so long," she had said.

It wasn't that his mother was sick or there was some problem at the store; they would have phoned. Barnsey's mind grew icy sharp. Everything was suddenly clear to him. He could see a trail of incidents leading to this if he thought about it. You just had to tilt life a bit, and there was a whole other picture.

His parents weren't very talkative. They didn't chatter; they didn't argue. And yet in the moments while his father unpacked the trunk of his salt-stained Mustang and made his way back and forth up the path Barnsey had shoveled so clean just the night before, Barnsey could hear in his head all the signs and hints stretching back through the months—how far, he wasn't sure. Right up to now, the past few days, with Grandma so attentive. Spoiling him rotten.

Then his father was in the living room, still in his coat, waiting for Barnsey to say something. His face didn't look good, but to Barnsey he didn't look anywhere near bad enough, all things considered. Grandma Barrymore was standing behind him with her hand on her son's shoulder. She looked very sad. They waited. Barnsey looked out the window. Old-fashioned lace curtains hung across the living-room window. They were always there, even when the drapes were open. Barnsey stood between the lace and the cold glass. He turned and looked at his grandma through the veil of the curtain.

"I wish you'd told me," he said.

"She didn't know, Matthew," said his father. "Not for sure."

The ball was back in his court. That was the way his parents were with him. Lots of room. His father would not press him. He could wait forever and his father would never start saying stuff like "I'm sorry, honey," or "It's all for the better," or "Your mother still loves you, Matthew." Barnsey could wait forever and he wouldn't see his father cry. He would have done his crying already, if he had any crying to do. His parents didn't hold much with spontaneity.

He glanced at his father in his black coat and white silk scarf. He wanted him to do something.

Barnsey stared out the window.

"When did you get the ski rack?" he said.

"When I needed something to carry skis."

There was a pair of skis on the top of the car. Rossignols.

"They're yours," said his father. "I couldn't exactly wrap them."

Barnsey had been wanting downhill skis. And one of the large boxes piled in the hall was probably a good pair of ski boots. His parents would have read consumer reports about this. Even while they were breaking up.

"Your mother is hoping maybe you'll go on a skiing trip with her later in the holidays. Maybe Vermont."

"That would be nice," said Barnsey. Then he left the window and went to his room. His father didn't follow. It was his way of showing respect. He didn't say that; he didn't have to. He was there for him. He didn't say that, either, but it was something Barnsey had heard often. "We're here for you, chum."

Barnsey stayed in his room a long time, long enough to hear both sides of the new X.P. tape he hadn't had time to listen to on the bus. He flipped the cassette cover again and again. The ghoul glowed and vanished. Glowed and vanished.

Then his mother phoned. They had probably worked all this out, too.

"Must have been a terrible shock . . .

"Decided it was best this way . . .

"We couldn't dissolve the partnership in time for the shopping season. . . .

"Couldn't see us play-acting our way through Christmas . . ."

Barnsey listened. Said the right things.

"Do you think we could head down to Mount Washington for a long weekend?" said his mother. "Give those new skis a workout?"

"They aren't new," said Barnsey.

"They sure are," said his mother. "They're the best."

"There's a lot of snow between here and Ottawa," said Barnsey. It took his mother a minute to realize it was a joke. A lame kind of joke.

Then, with plans tentatively set and the call over and his mother's voice gone, Barnsey joined his father and his father's mother in the living room. They both gave him hugs.

"You okay?" his father asked.

"Yes."

"You want to talk now? Or later?"

"Later," he said.

"I think we all need a sherry," said Grandma. She poured Barnsey a glass. He liked the idea better than the sherry.

They ate lunch and then, since it was Christmas, they sat in the living room opening presents. Barnsey kept glancing at his father, expecting to see a little telltale tear or something. But all he ever glimpsed were the concerned looks his father was giving him.

He took his father's place as the hander-outer. When he came to his own present for his mother, he said, "Where should I put this?" His father piled the package on a chair in the hall.

Barnsey wasn't looking forward to Christmas dinner at his aunt's. His father had already taken that into consideration and would stay with him at Grandma's, if he liked. They'd make something special, just the two of them. But when he phoned to explain things, his sister wouldn't hear of them not coming, and his cousins got on the phone and begged Barnsey to come and try out their new computer game and in the end he went. Nobody talked about his mother not being there, at least not while Barnsey was around. Everyone was really considerate.

In bed he lay thinking about what kind of a place his mother would live in. She was the one leaving the relationship, so she was the one leaving the house. Barnsey wondered whether there would be a room for him or whether she'd just make up a couch when he came to visit. Then he wondered if his father would stay in Ottawa or move back to the west coast. He tried to think what else could possibly go wrong. He didn't want any more surprises.

"I just wish someone had told me," he said.

"We'll turn it around, Matthew," his father had said when he came to say good-night. "We'll make this into a beginning."

Was that from some kind of a book? How could he

say that? Couldn't he tell the difference between a beginning and an ending?

There wasn't another man in his mother's life. His father hadn't found another woman.

"At least it isn't messy," his father said. He needn't have bothered. Nothing they ever did was messy.

In his sleep, Barnsey escaped. He found himself back on the bus.

"Rubbish," Dawn kept saying, and she pounded her fist into her palm every time she said it. Then the man in the seat ahead of them turned around, and it was the guy who had been in the country video heading home in his pickup through a blizzard to his tinsel-happy lady.

"Rubbish," he said. And then all of Xiphoid Process, who were *also* on the bus, turned around in their seats, pounding their fists and saying, "Rubbish. Rubbish. Rubbish." Soon the bus driver joined in and the whole bus sang a "Hallelujah Chorus" of "Rubbish, rubbish, rubbish."

Barnsey woke up, his head spinning. All he could think about was rubbish. He thought about the talk he had to have with his father that day. His father wouldn't insist, but he would be expecting it. He would say all the right things and, before Barnsey knew it, *he* would be saying all the right things, too. They'd talk it out. Get things out in the open. It would all make perfect sense.

Rubbish.

So he left.

He didn't pack a bag, only stuffed a couple of extra things in his backpack. He wasn't sure what a ticket

with Marsha there. Did he do it to impress her? Should I take off my shirt, too? If I did, would Marsha notice how pale my skin was next to his? On any other day. But it was one of those Sundays when nothing stupid mattered.

We reached the cedar woods that skirted the edge of the big swamp.

"Bet you a Ski-Doo's gone through," I said.

And Marsha said, "Didn't know you were a poet."

Nobody would take my bet. That's because we all knew there would be one. And, sure enough, there was a gaping hole in the ice halfway out, the snowmobile still sitting in it, prow high, water lapping up over the seat. It looked like some woebegone creature—a black pygmy hippo with yellow racing stripes. We stood watching it for a while, waiting for a dead body to float to the surface beside the machine. Nothing. You'd have to try pretty hard to drown in our swamp.

Last summer we came down here and MacDuffy led us, thigh-deep, through the muddy waters looking for snapping turtles. We filed behind him. We weren't afraid; he was an Indian. We didn't know that for sure—nobody had actually asked him—but he had black hair and dark skin and he knew stuff we didn't about things like the territories of red-tailed hawks. If he said he could catch us a snapper, then he could. He never bragged. Suddenly MacDuffy stopped and held up his hand. We didn't see anything, but we held our silence (and our crotches). What was it? Had he heard something? Had Snapper talked to him? No— bubbles. He followed them. Then with both hands he reached down, lightning quick so that the murky waters slopped against his chest, and came up with the biggest turtle I had ever seen. Its horny shell was as big as a serving platter. It reared its dinosaur head trying to take a piece out of MacDuffy's arm, while its legs tried to swim in the air. We waded ashore and watched it chomp sticks in half with its powerful jaws and beak. Then we let it go.

That turtle was somewhere out there now, sleeping under the mud, dreaming egg-shaped dreams.

As for the Ski-Doo—someone would come for it in a four-by-four with ropes and pulleys and a case of beer and probably a dog or two to bark a lot and get in the way. It was a tradition in these parts.

Marsha wanted to walk out to the Ski-Doo. The ice looked okay, and it probably was. But the snow around the edge wasn't. She went up to her knees in it. Freezing-cold muddy water poured into her boots. She grabbed onto me, and I pulled her out. Rugs got her boots. They came out with a sucking noise—*thuck!* He emptied out the water. By mistake he emptied out one of her socks, too. No one could find it.

"That's okay," said Greg. "I've got another one." He pulled a sock out of his pocket. He had an extra sock in his pocket. He didn't know why. We all laughed ourselves crazy. Then Marsha leaned against me while Greg wiped off her foot and put on the almost clean white sock.

"If this fits, you get to marry the prince," he said.

I stared hard at the Ski-Doo with Marsha leaning against me for support, trying not to lose my balance and sink like her missing sock into the gumbo. Did she look at me when Greg said that?

We reached the barn at last and found an old ladder in the long grass. We tried climbing it without leaning it against anything. MacDuffy said he was afraid of heights, but he smiled when he said it, so I couldn't tell if he was fooling. I got up two rungs; so did Marsha. Greg got up three. Rugs got to the fifth rung, but it broke and he fell fantastically with a loud splat into the melting snow. He laughed so hard that he couldn't get up. We all laughed and threw ourselves on our backs in the muck.

Then Greg thought of using the ladder as a stretcher. He and I jumped to our feet and piled Rugs on board. MacDuffy held Rugs down with a hand on his stomach and Marsha said she was the nurse and kept applying handfuls of snow to his forehead whenever he tried to sit up. We tore off around the barn with Rugs hanging on for dear life.

That's when we came upon the fox.

It was dead by the barn door, its snout full of porcupine quills.

"Probably rabid," said MacDuffy. "A fox isn't dumb enough to attack a porkster unless it's gone loco."

We let Rugs get up. We laid the ladder on the ground. How dazzling the fox was under the hot sun.

"Don't touch it," said MacDuffy. We knew that. Especially not its spit. There was spit all over its face. MacDuffy said we would have to phone the Ministry of Natural Resources. They would send someone up from the city and he would cut the fox's head off and take it back to town for testing.

"Why just the head?"

"That's where the disease is."

"Couldn't we just bury it?"

"No. Leave it."

Then Greg said, "I don't think so." And we looked up where he was pointing into the tall blue sky. There was a turkey vulture sailing on a thermal in a circle high above the barn. The first one of the season.

Using sticks, we loaded the fox onto the ladder-stretcher and carried it into the barn. Marsha cleared a flat spot and laid down a floor of old planks. The rest of us went looking for rocks. Careful not to touch the dead animal, we built a cairn of large stones over it. We filled in the cracks with smaller stones. Nothing could get at it now.

The barn sat on a knoll just up from an abandoned train bed. Rather than go back through the woods the way we had come, we walked along the train bed out to the division line.

We were quieter now. Wetter—that was part of it. But also there was the dead fox on our minds like a hot ember burning behind our eyes. In the quiet I could hear Marsha's boots squelching with every step. There were red strands in her brown hair—and gold ones. I'd never noticed that before. Shimmering.

I thought of as many words as I could to describe the way it looked:

Glittering.

Glimmering.

Gleaming.

Flickering.

Glinting.

I was so busy thinking about her hair that I didn't notice what the others did. Animal tracks. MacDuffy saw them first.

The animal tracks crossed the dirt division line that led back to my place, walked along the shoulder a ways, and then headed down into the woods on the east side of the road. They were bigger than any deer prints we had ever seen. An elk? A moose? We looked to MacDuffy for the answer.

Probably a moose.

This was thrilling. We squatted around a perfect footprint. A moose for sure. And if moose, then timber wolves next. And then the whole northern wilderness moving slowly southward.

"Makes sense," said Rugs. "All the factories in town are moving south to the States, Mexico."

His dad had lost his job the month before.

I imagined a flock of factories migrating overhead to warmer climes. And then I imagined lynxes and caribou and snowy owls coming to take their place.

Marsha picked up a fist-sized rock from the side of the road.

"We'll all become hunters and gatherers," she said.
"You'd better get quieter boots," I said.

It was the last leg of our trip and already growing
colder as the sun sank below the trees. With the sun
behind it we saw the ragged old truck sailing slowly
our way as if not powered by an engine at all. It was
the Considines. I didn't know them, but I knew their
truck. It was probably the oldest active vehicle in the
whole of the county. Considine couldn't get parts for
it anymore, so when something was broken, he made
it from scratch. My father said he had pretty well
rebuilt that truck part by part.

We watched the truck approaching as silently as a
ghost, a silhouette against the setting sun. They lost
a kid, the Considines. We all knew that. But none of
us knew exactly what that meant. Did it die at birth?
Had it gone through the ice? Did it die at all, or did
it just move to the city and forget to write? Or had they
left it outside the grocery store in its baby carriage and
it had ended up in Neverland like Peter Pan?

The truck rolled closer and we realized that Considine had turned the engine off, letting the long slow
hill carry them on down at its own speed. We waited
at the bottom.

Mrs. Considine rolled down the window. I had
never talked to them before. They weren't our kind
of people.

There was a dog on the front seat with them. It had
its head in a large bag of potato chips.

"You seen a cow?"

They had lost their cow. First their kid and now their cow.

A cow. Rugs was the first to get it. He hooted and slapped his leg. Then, at about the same moment, the rest of us got it.

We pushed MacDuffy up to the window. He looked sheepish. We kept shoving him in the back until he told the Considines about the "moose" tracks on the road.

The dog smelled MacDuffy's hand, licked it. Maybe he smelled fox. MacDuffy patted it. We all did. There was potato-chip dust all over the dog's muzzle. Mrs. Considine offered us some chips. Greg reached out to take some. Rugs grabbed his arm away.

"It's full of dog cooties."

Greg turned away as though he were going to be sick.

"No, thanks," said Marsha. Politely, for all of us. The rest of us were trying not to laugh. Greg was making barfing noises.

Mr. Considine started his engine. They thanked us for the information.

"With any luck those tracks'll lead us to Gloria," said Mrs. Considine.

The cow's name was Gloria.

We wandered the last bit of the way up the long slow hill, quietly swinging sticks, kicking at stones, looking for Gloria's tracks.

"I wish we could find that cow," said Marsha. She was walking beside me. "We could sell it for magic beans."

"Maybe the Considines would rather have a cow," I said. I knew I would rather have magic beans, but I wasn't sure about the Considines.

"Maybe they could plant a magic bean," said Marsha after she'd thought about it for a minute, "and climb the beanstalk and find their kid."

Sunday ended. That happens, though it wasn't easy to let it. But then some days taste so good they are like promises. I was supposed to study for a science test. I fell asleep after dinner with my textbook on my face.

I dreamed I was climbing a giant beanstalk. Marsha was just ahead of me.

The next thing I knew there was a dull morning light and my sister was bringing me a cup of tea. We take turns; it was her week. She was smiling from ear to ear. She pointed to the window. It was snowing. I was about to curse when I realized it was *really* snowing! Sitting up, I could see that the snow was up past the bumper of the car and blowing around crazily. There would be no bus, no school. It was winter's last gift.

Then, beyond the car in the woods, standing motionless in the trees as white and black as a snowy day, I saw the Considines' cow. Gloria. My sister raced for the phone. She came back a minute later. The Considines were on their way.

Then she sat wordlessly at the foot of my bed and we drank our mugs of tea. It was sweet—she always made it too sweet—but better than any other cup of tea I'd ever tasted. Every sweet, hot mouthful was like a taste of heaven.

TIM WYNNE-JONES is the author of several books for children as well as adult fiction, the book and libretto for an opera, and a children's musical. A children's book editor, he also writes music for his rock band, The Suspects. Mr. Wynne-Jones lives in eastern Ontario, Canada.

The Book of Changes features some of the same characters that appeared in the author's earlier collection, *Some of the Kinder Planets*, which was awarded the 1993 Governor General's Award for Children's Literature in Canada and which *Booklist* praised in a starred review as "wonderfully wise and witty stories . . . [that] deserve a place in both public and school library collections."